"Just what is Xena?"

Everyone who saw The Late Show with David Letterman *that night groaned at the host's vapid question. But Lawless, unfazed, batted her blue eyes and said, "Xena is a badass, kick-ass pre-Mycenaean girl who traverses the time lines . . . I can extract information from chaps by shutting off the flow of blood to the brain." She put her hands on Letterman's neck and mimed pressure on it as the audience roared its approval. In that moment, Lucy Lawless had joined the major leagues.*

This inside biography reveals the true story of Lucy Lawless—with details on . . .

- her wanderlust years traveling Europe

- her early acting days, including a role on TV's *Ray Bradbury Theater*

- her decision to perform her own stunts in *Xena: Warrior Princess*

- her struggle to balance her roles as mother and actress

- her aspirations to become a dramatic stage actress and more

LUCY LAWLESS, WARRIOR PRINCESS!
The Lucy Lawless Story

LUCY LAWLESS, WARRIOR PRINCESS!

Marc Shapiro

BERKLEY BOULEVARD BOOKS, NEW YORK

LUCY LAWLESS, WARRIOR PRINCESS!

A Berkley Boulevard Book / published by arrangement with
the author

PRINTING HISTORY
Berkley Boulevard edition / September 1998

All rights reserved.
Copyright © 1998 by Marc Shapiro.
Book design by Casey Hampton.
Cover design by Steven Ferlauto.
Cover photograph by Vinnie Zuffante / © Starfile Photo.
This book may not be reproduced in whole
or in part, by mimeograph or any other means,
without permission. For information address:
The Berkley Publishing Group, a member of Penguin Putnam Inc.,
375 Hudson Street, New York, New York 10014.

The Penguin Putnam Inc. World Wide Web site address is
http://www.penguinputnam.com

ISBN: 0-425-16545-0

BERKLEY BOULEVARD
Berkley Boulevard Books are published by The Berkley Publishing Group,
a member of Penguin Putnam Inc.,
375 Hudson Street, New York, New York 10014.
BERKLEY BOULEVARD and its logo are trademarks
belonging to Berkley Publishing Corporation.

PRINTED IN THE UNITED STATES OF AMERICA

10 9 8 7 6 5 4 3 2 1

This book is dedicated to . . .

the Warrior Women in my life: My wife, Nancy; my daughter, Rachael; my mother, Selma; and my agent, Lori Perkins. Also thanks for guidance to Bennie and Freda, who sit at the right hand of the gods. Ditto to Barry Neville, who forges the broadswords at Berkley. Thanks to the noise boys and girls—Kiss, Black Sabbath, Cirith Ungol, Patti Smith, and Charles Bukowski. Hell never sounded so good. And finally to the generations to come. Read and dream.

CONTENTS

ACKNOWLEDGMENTS

Celebrity Book Writing 101. Attention class! This is how *Lucy Lawless* was done.

Long distance. Lots of long distance. And I've got the phone bills to prove it. Burning up the lines between Pasadena, California, and Auckland and Wellington, New Zealand, resulted in a renewed fondness for the Kiwi. Not only were complete strangers, in places as far afield as the New Zealand Film Commission, the Auckland Theater Company, and a number of Auckland and New Zealand newspapers, willing to hear this Yank's blather; in many cases they willingly forked over further contacts and, in a couple of cases, actual home numbers of people in Lucy Lawless's life. On one occasion, the saint on the other end of a wrong number call offered to try local information for me and call back with the right number.

But don't get the idea that my long-distance relationship with New Zealand was a total love fest. A couple of people told me to stick it where the sun don't shine. But even one of those offered a valuable contact number in between attempts to bite my head off.

One need only look at the thank-you list at the end of this section to see that people were quite happy to talk about Lawless. In fact, the idea of somebody devoting an entire book to one of their own created a domino effect of enthusiasm as the likes of comics Willy de Wit and Dean Butler and cinematographer Wakka Atewell offered up valuable glimpses into Lawless's life, while others kicked in additional numbers and contacts and, in many instances, priceless information from Lawless's early television comedy stint with the group Funny Business.

Calls to Canada proved equally rewarding. The head of the William B. Davis Center for Actor's Study, *The X Files'* Cigarette Smoking Man William B. Davis returned my telephone message almost immediately, as did his teaching associate. Both added important flesh to the bones of Lawless's trip north for formal acting study. The people at Canada-based Atlantis Films were likewise cooperative in providing contact numbers for the producer, Mary Kahn, and director, John Reid, of Lawless's *Ray Bradbury Theater* appearance.

In the States, it took two calls to track down Douglas Wong, the martial arts trainer who taught Lucy Lawless to be a fighting woman, and only one call to hook up with actor Bruce Campbell.

The Internet (more about that in a later chapter) as always proved to be an invaluable source. Well over a hundred Web sites churned up information as well as newspaper and magazine articles that helped fill in the holes. An attempt was made to interview Lucy Lawless for this book, but she declined the request.

I would also like to thank the following publications and media outlets, which contributed information and insights into the life and times of Lucy Lawless: *Entertainment Weekly*, the *Los Angeles Times*, the *Rocket*, the *Virginian Pilot*, *TV Hits*, *New Zealand Women's Weekly*, *TV Guide*, *Yahoo*, the *Washington Post*, *Xena Media Review*, Knight Ridder Newspapers, *People Weekly*, *Cleo* magazine, *Starlog*, *Dreamwatch*, *Playboy*, *New Zealand TV Guide*, the *Dominion*, the *Scotsman*, the *Globe*, *Curve*, *Entertainment Tonight*, WGN TV, Sky TV, *Mr. Showbiz*, the *Vancouver Sun*, the *New York Post*, *Sci-Fi Universe*, Whoosh!, and the Lucy Lawless Fan Club.

And finally, to all the writers whose words have spread the word. They are Joe Nazarro, David Rensin, Ian Spelling, Mary Anne Cassata, James Brady, Karen S. Schneider, Kirsten Warner, Erik Knutzen, Rowan Wakefield, Ann Oldenburg, Lyle Harris, Mark Schwed, Mike Flaherty, Elizabeth Kastor, Neil Blincow, Candace A. Wedland, Gillian Gaar, Larry Bonko, Ward Morehoust III, Cathy Burke, Kim Farr, Gabrielle Stanton, Harry Werksman, Bret Ryan Rudnick, and Carmen Carter. Thanks. Let me know if I can return the favor.

Lucy Lawless . . . A Twist in the Tale

Pamela Anderson as Xena, Warrior Princess? Don't laugh. It could very easily have happened.

Because Hollywood is notorious for taking the easy way out when it comes to casting shows like *Xena: Warrior Princess*.

Certainly you don't look for the likes of Meryl Streep or Emma Thompson to be stepping into the role of a leather-miniskirted, sword-flailing, wise-cracking fighting woman anytime soon. But, on the other hand, you would hope against hope that, when studio executives sat down with producers over a three-martini lunch to cast Xena, they would look beyond the latest crop of bubble-headed, bleached bimbettes who had washed out of *Baywatch*.

Granted, *Xena* is not brain surgery in television form. Point of fact: this weekly slide into modified

Greek mythology is mind candy at its most fluffy. But it is candy that, from its inception, had a pedigree. *Xena* is smart in a comic book, nod-and-a-wink sort of way. It's hip in its execution and fun in the way that it flirts with camp. Consequently, *Xena: Warrior Princess* constituted an unusually complex and risky casting chore.

First and foremost you need a body in the role of Warrior Princess. Not just a great body but a body of . . . well, mythic proportions. Then you need somebody athletic—a woman who can ride a horse, wield a broadsword, and kick butt believably in an unbelievable world. Oh, and one more thing.

You need somebody who can act.

The reality in Hollywood is that you rarely get all three in the same package (again, witness *Baywatch*), and producers and studio types, when pushed into a corner, are likely to forgo the latter element in favor of the former two. Which is why, when complete unknown Lucy Lawless was thrown against the Universal Studios executive wall, she did not immediately stick. Lucy Lawless, in their eyes, was just too good to be true.

Here was somebody with body to burn, athletic prowess on the high side of extreme, and who was a real live actress who could emote beyond the blank-eyed zombie stare of somebody reading off a cue card. She was smart, she was determined, and she had a real world background that would put the narrow lives of most starlets to shame. And finally: She was not Pamela Anderson. In other words, Lucy Lawless was the complete package.

When Lawless was thrown into the hopper, the powers that be, unbeknownst to them, were also getting a bonus: Somebody who was not going to look down her nose at the role and who had a history of taking every part very seriously. *Xena: Warrior Princess* was not going to be high art. But Lucy Lawless was going to play it that way. If she got the role.

The studio top brass ultimately did the right thing. They looked beyond markers that needed to be called in, informal golf course deals, and the paybacks required to keep favored managers and agents happy. They cast the right person for the right role: Lucy Lawless.

That this book has been written stands as exhibit A to the fact that the right choice was made. You don't write biographies of actresses whose shows are laughably bad and get canceled after half a dozen episodes (not if you're sane). You don't burn up the telephone lines between the United States and New Zealand, digging up every scrap of info on an actress who will wind up in convention hell in a couple of years.

You do take the time to compile the most detailed biography possible of an actress who, in the space of three years, has gone from complete unknown to cult goddess and who is, as this book goes to press, already making non-Xenalike overtures toward a long-term career.

Personally, I would like nothing more than to have *Lucy Lawless: Warrior Princess!* avoid the fate of most celebrity books. I want this book to be around and viable ten years from now. In order for that to happen, Lucy Lawless has to have a career once she hangs up her leather miniskirt and her metal-studded bustier.

And, to be perfectly honest, I think she will.

ONE

One Break Leads to Another

Lucy Lawless hit the cement with a sickening thud. Lucy Lawless was in pain.

She heard the thudding of hooves as the horse stumbled and fell. If it fell to the left it would break every bone in her body. The horse's massive weight fell to the right.

Lawless lay sprawled motionless on her stomach. Somewhere in the back of her brain she heard the screams and terrified profanities. She turned her head slightly to the side as the stars began to disappear, just in time to see the late afternoon, Southern California sun blotted out by an army of concerned stunt coordinators, publicity people, and onlookers.

The voices grew louder. "Don't move her until we find out if anything's broken." But Lawless immediately knew something was not right. Her palms were raw and painful, as were various points on her arms and legs. She could feel the wetness that flowing blood brings.

And she could feel another sensation, a sharp, jagged throbbing from the area of her side and waist. Lucy Lawless had not heard anything snap. But it felt like broken bones.

Ever the trooper, Lawless attempted some self-deprecating remarks that ultimately turned into agonized curses as she attempted to shift her weight slightly to one side. Moments later a studio ambulance, always on hand when stunts were being attempted, rolled in and a couple of emergency medical technicians raced over and gave the actress a preliminary examination. The prognosis? Almost certainly something was fractured. More likely something was broken.

A collapsible gurney was immediately wheeled over and Lawless, as delicately as possible, was immobilized and stretched out on it. The gurney was raised and locked into place, and the actress was immediately wheeled into the ambulance. The doors closed, plunging Lawless and one of the attendants into semidarkness. Sirens began to wail as the ambulance pulled out, heading for a nearby hospital's emergency room. Inside, Lawless stared blankly up at the ceiling, silently cursing the fates. Her normally piercing blue eyes were clearly out of focus as she thought of how her daughter, Daisy, would react to the news, and laughed quietly, albeit painfully, at what this bit of foolishness had brought down around her head.

•   •   •

Lucy Lawless had been a more-than-willing partici- pant in the publicity machine that had brought her to the United States from New Zealand in late 1996 to help get the word out on her upcoming television se- ries, *Xena: Warrior Princess*. Perhaps it was naïveté or the idea that stardom had been a lucky break that deserved some payback; whatever the reason, Law- less, a statuesque, dark-haired, almost too beautiful to be true woman with sparkling blue eyes was more than willing to be the tacky foil for every "Good Morning," "Good Day," and "A.M." talk show in the country. Lawless dutifully cut loose with Xena's trademark warrior yell "Yi, yi, yi, yi!"; she dueled with plastic swords on a fairly regular basis; and she exhibited her singing background for the benefit of such hosts as Rosie O'Donnell.

"The media thing has been a little hard to get used to at times," she says, reflecting on her first adventure in the public eye. "But, by and large, people have been very good and very intelligent and I've been quite heartened by the way the TV programs have treated me and the show. They've actually been very kind and, at times, chivalrous."

Lawless quickly honed the fine art of talk show repartee, treating the most banal question or superfi- cial comment to a snappy comeback. She made major points with the public the night she appeared on *The Late Show with David Letterman*. Letterman, known far and wide for being unprepared and often quite uninterested in his guests, proved himself true to form when, moments after Lawless was introduced to a massive amount of applause, asked, "Just what is Xena?"

Lawless, not phased by the vapid question, came back with, "Xena is a badass, kick-ass pre-Mycenaean girl who traverses the time lines." The audience roared its approval.

Letterman, taken aback, continued his downward slide with the follow-up question, "Can she fly?" A smattering of groans rose from the knowledgeable members of the audience.

Lawless batted her blue eyes in a slightly innocent, slightly devilish way and leaned over the host's trademark desk. "No, I can't fly but, by the benefit of an Eastern acupressure technique, I can extract information from chaps by shutting off the flow of blood to the brain." She put her hands on Letterman's neck and mimed pressure on it as the audience roared its approval once again. In that moment, Lucy Lawless joined the major leagues.

And so when the nationally broadcast *Tonight Show* requested that, as part of her appearance, she film a skit in which she rides up to the studio in all her Xena finery astride a horse, Lawless did not blink an eye.

October 8, 1996

Lawless is gingerly dancing her horse back and forth in the NBC Studios lot in Burbank, California. A camera crew, standing nearby, is checking angles in preparation. Lawless is all smiles, and trades jokes with the handful of onlookers. After a final conversation with Lawless, the coordinator signals a rehearsal. Lawless eases her mount to the other side of the lot and begins a moderate gallop into frame.

Suddenly the horse lurches and skids on the pavement, sending Lawless flying over its head. The actress immediately throws her arms forward in a mostly unsuccessful attempt to cushion the blow. A moment later the horse totally loses its footing and topples over, scant feet away. "If it had fallen on me, it would have been a lot worse," Lawless will later explain.

No, Xena is not invincible. But given the overnight success of *Xena: Warrior Princess* and the giant step from total obscurity to total stardom that has been the lot of its star Lucy Lawless, it's easy to see why the impression at large is that nothing mortal could lay the actress low.

Xena is a mixmaster of fighting women images ranging from Wonder Woman to Barbarella to Red Sonja, and is in the best pop-culture/pulp tradition, all things to all people. In general, there's the appeal of this big, strapping, attractive Amazon wandering mythological lands, righting wrongs and kicking ass with wildly exaggerated acrobatics and speaking with a tongue that wavers between the lilt of Shakespeare and the drawl of a street punk.

But all these elements would mean little without sex, and in the five-foot-ten-inch, thirty-year-old Lawless, Xena has the perfect embodiment of a free spirit who flaunts her sexuality in a number of sly ways, an aspect that reviewers were quick to pick up on. One of the most obvious came from the *Washington Post*, whose reviewer wrote, "You will immediately notice her breasts. Really there's no way not to what with all the swirls and twists of metal buttressing her leather bustier. And the thighs, long and muscular beneath the flaps of her leather miniskirt."

While the reviewer was obviously in heat, he was not far off in his assessment of Xena as a sexual animal. No virgin this Amazon; the show goes to great and not-so-subtle lengths to show that Xena has the attention of men. And, with her sidekick and confidant, Gabrielle, the show has produced moments that hint at the possibility of lesbian relationships. One need only look to the episode in which Xena plants a big, wet, full-mouthed kiss on Miss Known World beauty pageant winner Miss Artiphys to realize how far the show and Lawless are willing to go. That the contest winner turned out to be a drag queen seemed to make perfect sense in the mixed-up mythology where Lawless holds court.

"Xena's got the devil on her shoulder," Lawless has said. "That's why people are watching her because you never know which way she will jump. But she's not about T&A and she's not about flesh. Xena is a woman who fights for what she believes in. But, ultimately, Xena is totally unlike me."

Feminist icon. Lesbian fantasy and ultimate babe for the boys. It's no wonder that Xena—and Lawless—has become the latest object of cult worship in some mighty divergent quarters. Internet Web sites, straight, gay, and all points in between, devoted to all things Lawless and Xena have sprung up like weeds.

Meow Mix, a lesbian bar in New York, began having regular *Xena* nights in which the regulars would shout and moan at *Xena* episodes and engage in swordplay with plastic swords in a very *Rocky Horror* kind of way. A Web page think tank called the International Association of Xena Studies serves as one of the better clearinghouses for the latest Xena/Lawless info, as does the very hip on-line mag *Xena Media Review*. And, as befitting any pop-culture tidbit that begins the climb into the rarefied atmosphere of *Star Trek* and *The X-Files*, there is merchandise to burn. With less than three full seasons in the can, *Xena: Warrior Princess* has arrived and the reasons are as varied as the people you talk to.

"I watch her in action and think 'Wow! she could kick my ass! and I kind of dig that,' " enthuses an on-line regular known only as George. "Xena's a total babe who likes other babes. It's a babe fest!"

"It's sort of like old *Star Trek*," states International Association of Xena Studies chairperson Kym Masera Taborn. "It's so off-the-wall and seems so cut off from everything."

Lawless, never at a loss for a one-liner, once indicated that a big chunk of her following was "fifty-five-year-old lawyers who want to be spanked."

But while Xena is strictly the stuff of dreams, Lucy Lawless's coming of age in the role has not exactly been a fairy tale. Her eight-year marriage to husband Garth Lawless ended, literally, on the eve of her debut as Xena. And playing Xena has caused some emotional rifts between herself and daughter Daisy as the ravages of celebrity have blurred the lines between mom and superstar. And Lawless has made more than her share of tabloid headlines, in particular when, not too long after her divorce, she took up with *Xena* producer Rob Tapert, effectively—according only to unnamed sources in the tabloids—wrecking Tapert's long-running common law relationship with a screenwriter.

"It's been difficult on a lot of fronts," concedes Lawless. "I've gone through a lot of changes and so have the people around me. But we're managing."

The consensus is that Lawless is not only managing but thriving in her star status. Director Michael Levine, who piloted Lawless's fortunes in four episodes of *Xena*, remarks, "I think Lucy is more real people than a lot of celebrities."

"There are people who you don't wish success because of their attitude," recalls Willy de Wit, a member of the New Zealand comic troop Funny Business, in which Lawless cut her acting teeth. "I've never heard anybody say Lucy didn't deserve that. In this business there's luck and there's talent and then there's a combination of both. I think the last is definitely Lucy."

"I was sure she was a person who was going to, somehow, make it," remarks William B. Davis, her teacher during an acting school stint in Canada. "There's so much chance in this business and you never really know how things are going to fall out. But I always suspected that things would work out for Lucy."

Garry Davey, another acting teacher, had this reaction when informed that Lawless had landed the role of Xena: "Holy cow! That's neat!"

Actor Bruce Campbell, who appeared opposite Lawless in the *Xena* episodes "The Royal Couple of Thieves" and "The Quest" and who is never at a loss for a pithy assessment, describes Lawless's rise to pop stardom this way: "Lucy is an actress who just stumbled her way into the wacky world of Hollywood. It just hit her like a freight train. But given how lucky she's been, it turned out that she really has the stuff and packs one hell of a punch."

The ambulance carrying Lawless rounds a corner and pulls to a stop in front of the emergency room entrance. The doors swing open and Lawless is wheeled into the emergency room proper. This early on a Tuesday night, only a few scattered patients see Lawless being carted in. If they know who she is, they choose not to acknowledge the star in their midst. A brief conversation between the EMTs and the emergency room doctor follows as Lawless is taken into a curtained-off area and gingerly lifted onto a bed.

Some preliminary prodding and poking is followed by a quick trip down the hall to the X ray department. A short time later, the attending physician comes back with the news that Lawless has suffered a fracture of her pelvis.

Lawless sighs. Tears, born of frustration and the still throbbing pain, begin to well up in her eyes. The fall will require a number of days' hospital stay and a lot of bed rest. For a while she will be just plain Lucy Lawless again. Which will give her plenty of time to think about the future.

And the past. . . .

TWO

Rough Diamond

Frank and Julie Ryan loved children. It showed in their house, a veritable maze of child-friendly hideaways and hallways ideal for long runs, built on a small rise in the tiny town of Mount Albert, south of Auckland, New Zealand. It showed in the climate of mild temperatures and temperate sea breezes that made Mount Albert a year-round playground for running, jumping, and swimming in the nearby lakes and ocean.

And finally it showed in that, as good Catholics, Frank and Julie Ryan were destined to have children. Lots of children. Julie Ryan became pregnant with the couple's first child soon after they married. It was a boy. In the ensuing years Julie would give birth to three more boys.

When Julie became pregnant for the fifth time in

1967, the smart money, in gossip sessions around town, was on a fifth boy joining the growing Ryan clan. Frank and Julie, as was their manner, only hoped for a healthy baby. But, if pressed, both confessed that a little girl would be nice.

Lucy Ryan was born on March 29, 1968, a squirming bundle with piercing blue eyes. "She was the first girl after four boys," recalls Frank Ryan. "Lucy immediately became a very special child to us."

Lawless, years later, jokingly reflected on her parents' propensity for having a large Catholic family— for, in fact, a younger brother and sister eventually followed Lawless into the world. "There was a lot of traffic for one womb," she cracked. "But then, that was quite the standard family in Mount Albert. I do know that, after four boys, they were kind of relieved to see me turn up."

The young Lucy Ryan was a quick study when it came to growing up in a house full of older brothers. She remembers a household punctuated by "lots of squabbling and a general sense of chaos" and recalls that while the feeling she had from an early age was "of a real good, loving home," there was also an ingrained spirit of competitiveness that, although unspoken, was very much a part of the young child's formative years.

"You had to be kind of tough to survive in my home," remembers Lawless of those early years. "We were a highly competitive family when it came to things like sports. I had four older brothers who were not going to give an inch so it went without saying that, from the time I could walk, I was going to have to keep up.''

Consequently, among the earliest memories the people of Mount Albert have of her is as a three-year-old Lucy Ryan running after her brothers in the front yard and streets adjacent to the family bungalow, falling down and skinning her knees and elbows but then getting to her feet and taking out after them again.

''I was a tomboy,'' Lawless has said of her wonder years. ''My mother always used to say that I didn't know I was a girl until I was eight years old because nobody told me. I think there was a lot of natural aggression in me even though it was something I didn't really recognize at the time. Growing up with five brothers, it was pretty much the law of the jungle. I had to learn how to wheedle and manipulate to get what I wanted. I had to learn how to keep coming back from the knocks and the falls. It was a very loving home and everything but it was still a very rowdy environment.''

Ryan, dubbed ''a rough diamond'' by her parents, was also quick to mix it up when the Ryan clan would get into neighborhood games with children from the surrounding streets.

''The neighborhood kids would go down to the field behind our house,'' recalls Lawless's father, ''and have these great battles, throwing grass clippings and rotten fruit at each other. Lucy would always be right there, giving it her best. She had a great throw and a good, strong arm. She learned early on to give as good as she got.''

A younger brother and sister eventually came

along, swelling the Ryan family to seven children. Lucy, however, adjusted well to younger siblings, looking on the new arrivals as just additional play-mates rather than rivals to be jealous of. In fact, for a middle child, Lawless was made conspicuous by her even-tempered, albeit spirited nature. "She was a lovely little kid," states her mother. "She never caused any trouble."

Nor did she make any secret, at a very early age, that performing was in her blood. She would, by age five, regularly proclaim to anyone who would listen that "I want to be rich and famous."

Lucy's parents would always smile when their daughter made that pronouncement, assuming that life would discourage what they perceived as an unreal-istic goal. Besides, family history seemed to indicate that Lucy would eventually drop the fantasy in favor of something more practical. The Ryans, with the ex-ception of a great-grandmother, had long made their way as either politicians or lawyers. Her father, who became mayor of Mount Albert the year Lucy was born and held the job for the better part of twenty years, stood out as a perfect example. "It was always kind of like the big joke in the family when she would say things like that," recalls her father. "It was just like one of those things you would expect a young child to say."

But her mother reflects on the fact that Lucy, even at her most rough-and-tumble, seemed to have an in-nate theatrical sense about her that could turn even the most mundane children's game into literally a three-ring circus.

"No matter what she would be doing, it would always seem to end up in a performance," says Julie. "I'll never forget the little gymnastics displays and dramas she used to put on with her friends. It was like a regular event in the neighborhood. The kids would be out in the front yard, usually with Lucy organizing some bit of business, and the neighbors would all have to come out and watch.

"She was also quite the little athlete. In fact she learned to do a lot of the flips she does now as Xena on our bed. The children would all gather by our toilet and open the door so they could get a running start and then run across the house and tumble onto our bed. Lucy was real enthusiastic about it and would do all these tumbles and rolls and all kinds of flips."

And when she was not doing gymnastics, Lucy would slip into a world where she was a famous singer. Her mother relates that Lucy "would get up on our coffee table with a seashell for a microphone and just sing away." Lawless, looking back years later, laughingly recalled her own memories of childhood high jinks. "I used to take my mom's scarves, tuck them into my leotards, and dance around, doing the ballet to some really awful music."

Lawless, by her own account, "always had this bug to perform. . . . I was also very much a precocious kid, which kind of added to a sense of the theatrical that seemed to follow me around, even at an early age. It just seemed like I was born with the knowledge of what I wanted to do."

And in their own straightforward, New Zealand way, Lawless's parents let her know that they would be behind her no matter what her life decision might be. "My parents were tremendously supportive. There was this kind of unspoken bond that was strong with both my parents but especially with my dad. He let me know early on that there were no bonds on me."

Lawless began her formal education at age five in the local Mount Albert public school system, where a maturity beyond her years began to emerge. Yes, she was still the cutup and could be counted on to be at the center of any schoolyard happening. But there was also a sense of purpose in the young Lawless that caught the eye of teachers and adults who were witness to the ways of the youngster for the first time. It came as no surprise to her mother.

"Lucy was very sensible at a very early age," acknowledges Julie Ryan. "She was always very grown-up in her manner. I remember one of the mothers of Lucy's playmates telling me that she felt that Lucy was never a child."

Lawless's public school education lasted only a couple of years before she entered the first of a string of religious and convent-affiliated schools. Catholicism as a way of life was already an important part of the young girl's upbringing. She admits to having been "affected by religion in a positive way" from the beginning. She did not have to be dragged to church and, in fact, would have almost perfect attendance at the Mount Albert congregation until the age of eighteen.

"Catholicism gave me a real sense of mortality at a very early age," she has recalled of her strict but uncharacteristically "liberal" upbringing. "I knew that there was death and that, at some point, I was going to die. But it did not so much distress me as it made me in an awful hurry to get on with my life, to achieve and to soak up as much life as I possibly could."

It had become apparent by the time she had reached age eight that Lawless was going to be a big girl. By the third school year, the young girl was already standing head and shoulders above a good many of her classmates. But, while there was the expected teasing, Lawless seemed to take it in stride and, as her mother recalls, appeared quite comfortable with her stature. "Certainly Lucy was tall. But she was never ungraceful. She carried herself quite well."

Given the rather rigid approach of her Catholic school education, it is surprising to note that the young Lawless's penchant for theatrical turns seemed to thrive rather than wilt during her early school years. "At around age eight or nine I discovered how cool it was to be the class dunce," recalls Lawless with a chuckle. "Part of it was just the way I was and part of it came from the fact that I discovered that you could get away with quite a bit by pretending to be a dummy."

And part of it was the desire to act that was slowly but surely making its way to the surface. "I suppose with my childhood singing and dramas, I always had it in my head that I would act," admits Lawless. "I don't think I really ever entertained doing anything else."

But to that point there had never been a formal

outlet for Lawless's nascent abilities. At least not until, at age ten, her grade-school class mounted a dramatized version of the prodigal son.

"I played the woman who meets the prodigal son on the road and stiffs him out of his coins and clothes. I was the tough broad even then. When I was up in front of everybody, saying the words and doing these scenes in such a grand fashion, it felt very good inside. We were halfway through the play and I realized that I really liked this. After the play was over, I was standing out in the hallway and I was just so excited. That's when I made the decision that I was going to be an actor."

Ryan's acting aspirations were fueled by her mother's charity work. "My mother was involved in entertaining this senior citizens' group every week and she would rope a friend of mine and myself into helping her out with singing and dancing and skits."

Lawless grew from precocious child to preteen with her vision mostly intact. During her seventh year at Wesley Intermediate School, the young girl began to dream of a future beyond the limits of Mount Albert. Part of this imagined future lay in the more practical, responsible world, and manifested itself as a short-lived interest in marine biology and pathology.

"I don't think I gave either occupation any real consideration," said Lawless when reminded of those childhood goals. "I wanted to be a marine biologist because the name sounded good and I wanted to be a pathologist because Quincy, M.D., on the television was one."

But there was also a strong fantasy side that was

never far from her thoughts. "I began to fantasize about how, someday, I was going to go to Europe and pick grapes off the vine. The idea just sounded so romantic to me at the time." But her early teen years were occupied with more than just dreams. Lawless discovered that her childhood attempts at singing had flowered into a pretty decent voice and, when she was not belting out accompaniment to the pop hits of the day, she began thinking seriously about a career as a singer.

Lost in the growth spurt, however, was her childhood athletic prowess. "I guess I just grew out of it," remembers Lawless. "I was never a sports freak or anything like that. In fact my nickname in school was 'Unco' or 'Uncoordinated.' "

Lucy Ryan was voted most likely to succeed during her seventh year at Wesley Intermediate School. For her father, Frank, that was an indication of greater things to come for his first daughter. "That was the moment when Lucy's mother and I realized that she had the ability to do whatever she chose to do."

Ryan matriculated to Marist Sisters' College for her high school years in early 1982. By this time the young girl's life had become a full plate of studies, theatrical endeavors . . . and boys.

"Lucy was always very popular with the boys," recalls her mother. "She would get all the telephone calls. When it came to dating and such, she was always treated with great respect. There was never any nonsense and we were never let down by her."

There was, by contrast, a definite sense of urgency and excitement when Lucy, not yet fifteen, began to appear in her high school drama department's productions. Her performances in such productions as *The Macado*, *South Pacific*, and *The Pirates Of Penzance* were highlighted by her sparkling renditions of the famous numbers featured in those classic musicals. "She had a fine singing voice," says her father, well known in the town of Mount Albert for his ability to state his case in a few words. "And it was something that we encouraged."

To the extent that, when Lucy turned fifteen, she was rewarded with a European holiday. "It was a tour of all the big opera houses," reports Lawless. "I saw things like *Carmen* a million times. But it turned out to be an amazing experience that really awakened my senses."

Lucy returned from Europe energized with the possibilities of a singing career. She immediately enrolled in opera classes while continuing to pursue what she perceived as her very realistic goal of becoming a film and television star. Yes, there was indeed a lot on this fifteen-year-old's plate.

Lucy's room during her teen years spoke volumes about the pragmatic head on the young girl's shoulders. Whereas the walls of her girlfriends' rooms were plastered floor to ceiling with posters and magazine cutouts of the latest pop music and television stars, Lucy's walls were made conspicuous by their lack of such decoration.

"I never really went in for heroes as a teenager. I never put posters up of anyone and I wasn't particularly interested in pop culture. All my heroes at that time were real people . . . like my mum and dad."

Lawless credits this lack of fantasy hero worship to the progressive social climate that seemed part and parcel of New Zealand at the time. "Women, as near as I could see, were never made to feel disadvantaged in our country. The attitude when I was growing up was that anybody could be anything they wanted. Which is why I never longed to see a woman superhero. I just never felt disadvantaged in my own life."

Lucy graduated from high school in 1985 and immediately found herself at a crossroads. Her passion for acting and opera remained intact. She was also feeling a gnawing inside—a bad case of wanderlust that did not end at the Mount Albert city limits.

While attempting to sort things out, Lawless took a job busing tables at the local drinking-man's club, Club Mirage. It was there that she made the acquaintance of the eighteen-year-old head bartender, Garth Lawless. Like most of the lads of Mount Albert, Lawless was cut from blue-collar cloth; big on sports and working with his hands. But there was also a sweet soul in this salt-of-the-earth young man that, when combined with a real sense of spontaneity and living for the moment, appealed to Ryan's budding wild side.

Lucy was cautious at first. She was concerned that this budding first love would ultimately put up a roadblock to her escaping the confines of Mount Albert. But, finally, she gave in to his persistance and the pair formed an easygoing love match.

THREE

Road Rules

Enrolling at Auckland University in 1986 seemed like the logical first step in Lucy's flight to freedom. Auckland was near enough that she could keep family ties, as well as regular visits with Garth, within her grasp. But Auckland, the closest thing to a thriving metropolis in New Zealand, was also different enough to expose her to an urban energy that she knew, in her heart of hearts, she needed in a very real way.

And for the first few months at Auckland University, Lucy's expectations were met. She was around a more cosmopolitan crowd, hanging out in hip college places, and she was having her operatic singing and theatrical talents honed by a more progressive brand of educators. In line with her newfound interest in education, Lucy plunged headlong into language studies, including German but becoming particularly proficient in French and Italian. She also began to practice the emotionally and spiritually freeing art of yoga.

Eventually, however, though her grades were quite good and she rarely skipped a class, she began to lose interest in what this amount of freedom was bringing her. If her teachers and campus chums could have gotten behind those eyes, they would have seen that Lucy Ryan's mind was definitely on other things.

"I was still very much into acting. At that point I didn't entertain anything else seriously. I was still into opera singing and, at that point, I seemed to have a certain rough talent for it. But I didn't seem to have enough love for it and the life. I just didn't have the passion anymore," Lucy explains. "I was still in New Zealand and New Zealand was still a small country. And, when you come from a small place like New Zealand, you have to get out and eat up the world."

Lucy turned eighteen in 1987 and, with her wanderlust kicking into high gear, dropped out of Auckland University for what would turn out to be nearly a year-long voyage of discovery. Her parents, in keeping with their liberal disposition, were somewhat comfortable and supportive of her decision. From her father came the inevitable warnings to be careful and watch who she met up with. From her mother came more words of caution, a few tears at the prospect of her daughter venturing off into the unknown, and a parting gift.

"My mother made me take this big, ugly, yellow

suitcase." Lawless laughs at the memory. "It was like a millstone around my neck."

Lucy still had the vision of picking grapes on the Rhine and so it came as a surprise to her family when she impulsively decided on Lucerne, Switzerland, as her first stop outside of New Zealand soil.

"I was desperate to escape my claustrophobic family, my small country, and just have a wild life. What I discovered when I got to Lucerne was that it was hardly the wildest place on earth and was actually a very moral place. It was not the sort of place to go to have a cathartic, teenage rebellion."

Next stop: Prague, where Lucy often found a tonic for her bouts of loneliness in a place called Players' Park. "I would go there and see free plays. They were rubbish, they were the worst. I remember one play being put on in the park by some Canadian students in which people were hitting each other over the head with big mutton chops and screaming about the Plague. After sitting and watching things like that for a while, I decided I was not as miserable as I thought I was."

Truth be known, Lucy was not miserable at all during this first phase of her odyssey. The idea of being a vagabond on the road to who knows where with a knapsack on her back and very few material possessions and even less money seemed to appeal to the vision of unbridled freedom she had formed in her head. But she does concede to some real moments of doubt.

"It was a big cold world out there," she recalls with no small degree of relish. "Those were danger-

ous days because I had no money, I was young, and
I didn't know anybody. I was sleeping where I could
and I was living on coffee and cigarettes until I was
almost skeletal. But I was too proud to cave in and
ask for help from my parents. It was one big adventure for me. And besides, I was convinced that there
was nothing much for me to be afraid of. It's hard to
die even when you have no money, nothing to eat,
and nowhere to sleep.''

Lucy, while soaking up the bohemian life, kept up
a steady correspondence with Garth Lawless.
Through letters, postcards, and the rare telephone call,
they discovered that absence did indeed make the
heart grow fonder. As Lucy was making ready to head
for the Rhine in Germany to fulfill her childhood
grape-picking fantasy, Lawless vowed to meet her
there. Lucy arrived in Germany right around the time
Garth, true to his word, came shambling into town.
But rather than picking grapes, the pair soon found
other diversions.

''When I finally got to Germany, the romance of
grape picking on the Rhine kind of went out the window,'' she says, laughing. ''I would be hanging out
in coffee shops and bars with some rather questionable types. It was a lot of fun. But, with no money
coming in, eventually I had no money at all.''

The answer to Lucy's dilemma came in the guise
of her always quick-thinking boyfriend's sense of dra-
matics and twisted logic. ''Garth came up with quite
a tactic.'' Lawless chuckles at the memory. ''He said,
'Let's go to Australia, earn a bit of money, go back
to Europe, and then travel to Russia.' I couldn't think

of a better idea and we were down to it on funds, so I said why not?''

But before they went to Australia Lucy and Garth spent a final dalliance in Greece, where they hung out and watched their funds run out. They arrived penniless in Australia and in need of a job. With the specter of a Russian holiday and more adventures ahead, the pair agreed that they needed to make a lot of money in a short period of time. Which ruled out more traditional forms of employment. But not romantic ones.

''For me the notion of gold mining was as romantic as the idea of grape picking was,'' she notes. ''I liked the idea of being down underground with this light on my head, picking chunks of gold out of the soil.''

However, when the pair signed on to mine gold in the Australian Outback, Lucy's pleasantly idealized fantasy soon gave way to reality. They had been hired by a gold mining operation in the tiny town of Kalgoorlie, approximately five hundred miles from the city of Perth. After a short period of instruction in the fine art of getting gold out of the ground, they were relocated to an even smaller mining operation, two hours' drive from the outskirts of Kalgoorlie.

What immediately caught Lucy's eye upon arriving at the desolate mining camp was the sheer isolation of the place. Dust, dirt, and desert scrub dotted the landscape as far as the eye could see. Living quarters were more shanty than château. And the miners she would work with, primarily men and a few women, may have been handsome and beautiful, but it was hard to tell with the seemingly permanent coat of dust that turned exposed skin a rusty brown and obscured expressions and faces.

Any hope that mining in the Australian Outback would have some romance attached to it disappeared that first morning when Garth and Lucy were rousted out of bed before the sun came up. "That whole Seven Dwarfs thing went out the window for me that first day," she remembers. "I found out that the reality was drilling deep holes, pouring in explosives, and watching the whole mess go up in a bloody atomic blast that lays waste the landscape."

What Lucy also discovered was that in this equal rights profession, she was expected to do everything the men did, which, in her case, meant digging in the mines, mapping the ground, driving trucks, changing tires when those trucks ran over spikes, and pushing huge core samples of earth through diamond saws. "It was grueling, bloody awful work," she recalls. "But it was good, honest work and there was the advantage of going home at the end of the working day laden down with gold nuggets that we'd picked up."

As it turned out, men on this isolated outpost outnumbered women fifty to one. Being with Garth tended to defuse any sexual tension and even when alone, Lawless remembers being more than capable of fending off unwanted advances.

"I had heard all kinds of verbal abuse and smart-aleck comments when I was growing up and so, even when the miners came on to me that way, I was able to give back as good as I got. But, for the most part, the miners were fine with me.

"I never had any trouble and I think the main reason was that I never attracted any unwanted attention," she continues. "I was careful to not put out any vibes that indicated I was looking for that kind of attention. I knew I didn't want a pack of randy miners on my tail and so I took the necessary precautions to not have any unhappy accidents. Obviously I wasn't walking around with my bum and boobs hanging out all the time. It's only an unhappy accident if you get yourself in trouble and I did not want any accidents or trouble."

The days tumbled together, a blur that lasted well into 1987. The couple acknowledged Lucy's nineteenth birthday with a couple of brews. Most days Lucy and Garth barely had the strength to crawl back to their place and soak their aching muscles and bruised arms and legs, stroke their cat, Basil, and gaze out at the occasional kangaroo whose quick pass through the Outback landscape was considered a major break with monotony. It was a rough experience but one that Lawless laughingly recalls was paying dividends. "We ended up making quite a lot of money, for people with no talent and no degrees."

In fact Lucy and Garth were counting the days until they would hop a plane for Russia, when Lucy turned up three months pregnant. It did not come as a complete surprise to Lawless. She knew she had missed a couple of periods but attributed the disruption of her cycle to the strenuous line of work she had suddenly undertaken. And, to be honest, she knew that she and Garth had been tempting the fates by having sex.

Needless to say the trip to Russia was off.

"When I found out I was pregnant, we just kind of sat and stared at each other for a moment," relates Lawless. "Finally we decided, 'Hey! Here's a really cool idea! Let's get married!' "

The marriage ceremony, conducted in an Outback town registry office, a stiflingly hot, poorly ventilated cement building, was more comic than serious but seemed to go part and parcel with Lucy and Garth's way of rampaging through life.

"It was crazy." Lawless chuckles at the memory of her magic moment. "The two witnesses at our wedding had these children who were screaming throughout the entire ceremony. I wore my sixth-grade ball dress. I don't know why I took that dress with me from home but I had it on hand and it was the closest thing to a wedding gown that I had. And then, because I was three months pregnant, I couldn't get the damned thing to fit. It was a pretty sorry exercise."

But one that Lucy, at the time, was able to put the best face on.

"The way we went about things was obviously not right," she concedes. "But at the time things appeared to have worked out for the best."

FOUR

Lucy Goes Big

The ink had hardly dried on the marriage certificate when Lucy, now a nineteen-year-old blushing bride, and Garth hopped a plane and left the land down under for the land not quite so under, New Zealand, in particular, Auckland.

Given their footloose ways, and the fact that they had managed to save quite a bit of money from their gold-mining adventures, the new Mr. and Mrs. Lawless probably could have settled anywhere. But Lucy's sense of family, now magnified by the life growing steadily in her belly, inspired her to settle within hailing distance of Mount Albert.

Lucy had been concerned how her parents, given their strict Catholic convictions, would react to the pregnancy and the rushed marriage and so she had already called from Australia with the news that yes, she was pregnant and yes, she and Garth were getting married. The reaction was equal parts disappointment, at the out-of-wedlock conception, and relief that plans had already been made to legitimize the child. But by the time Lucy and Garth's plane touched down at the Auckland airport, any disappointment dissolved amid a swarm of hugs, kisses, and stomach pattings.

The adventure was over. It was now well into 1987 and so Lucy and Garth set about getting on with their lives.

The couple found a tiny apartment on a rather spartan street on the outskirts of Auckland. Life in the flat of the Grey Lynn section of Auckland was never boring. Lucy and Garth were crowded into a one room flat. In other rooms were a struggling writer, a former women's basketball star and a trampoline coach. It was not the perfect place, as Lucy recalls. "We were surrounded by mad old ladies with cats," she groans. "They quite nearly drove me insane."

Garth quickly found work, managing a nearby workingman's bar. Lucy, by now well into her fourth month, was not only showing but afflicted with bouts of morning sickness. What she also discovered was that the urge to act, which had been temporarily put on a back burner during their jaunt through Europe and Australia, was now close to the surface again.

"I found I still had this irresistible urge to perform," she remembers. "But I was obviously in no condition to do much except dream about it. I was going to be a mother and Garth had buckled down and was being real responsible and supportive. I had a lot more to think about at the time than acting."

It was at this point that Garth and Lucy made the acquaintance of budding filmmaker Wakka Attewell. Money was tight, so whenever the trio would get together it was usually at some low-end restaurant or café. And it was during these informal get-togethers that Attewell formed a definite impression of the young couple.

"They were definitely people of the earth," he reflects. "I saw them as being a bit naïve. I think they were at a point when things were coming thick and fast and that they were simply in search of a lifestyle that suited them."

Lucy went into labor that same year and gave birth to a baby girl named Daisy. Lucy's mothering instincts were immediately evident. She was never far from Daisy's side and would literally drop everything at the first cry. Lucy, questioned at the time, could find no loftier a goal than motherhood. But, in hindsight, she admits that Daisy had no sooner popped into the world than her mind was on acting—and in the worst way.

"The week that I had my baby, I got real fired up to get on with it [acting]. I didn't know exactly how I would go about doing it but I did know that I had to go out and make something happen."

And she was determined, even at that point, to put everything she had into it.

"I wanted to be a fine actress, a really fine actress. I did not aim to just be mediocre. I wanted to be at the top of my profession and I knew it would be a lifelong odyssey to get to that level."

Going through her mind as she attempted to sort

out her attack on the imposing walls of stardom was
whether or not she should use her maiden name of
Ryan or adopt some imaginary moniker. The idea of
simply going out as Lucy Lawless made her wince.
"I kind of fancied the name of Lawless when I first
got married," she has reflected. "But then I thought,
Who is going to take me seriously as an actress with
this name."

She finally decided, in a typically Lucy turn of bra-
vado, that she would sink or swim as Lucy Lawless.
The only question was in what role would she take
that first tentative plunge.

She finally decided that she needed to get something down on film and so, with the aid of her be-
mused family and friends, she wrote a number of
skits, starring herself, and filmed them. This crude
form of self-promotion featured Lawless in a series
of almost burlesque comedies that, embellished with
some props and goofy situations, seemed created for
the sole purpose of allowing Lucy to rattle off lame
but enthusiastic one-liners that, fortunately, never
made it beyond an audience of immediate family
members and a few curious neighbors. Lucy, ever the
realist, knew that what she had committed to film was
not high art.

"They're kind of embarrassing," she concedes.
"But they were kind of funny. At least they showed
I had the guts to go out and do something really hid-
eous in order to·make something happen."

Garth Lawless, perhaps more as a concession to
new motherhood and still scrambled hormones, was
encouraging. He saw in Lucy somebody caught up in

the very kind of fantasy that had propelled their adventures in Europe and Australia. He could not deny her this round of giggles when she was being the devoted wife and mother, knowing that reality would hit Lucy soon enough and that she would cut out her wild ways and settle for domestic bliss. Lucy, for her part, was appreciative of Garth's going along with her wild notions. "He was being supportive," she recalls. "He would never say no. I appreciated that."

Lucy, when not finding Daisy a loving handful, persisted in her attempts to enter the New Zealand acting community, which, at the time, was small and tough to crack into.

Eventually she graduated from home movies to acting classes where, under the guidance of professional actors and teachers for the first time, she caught their attention with an enthusiasm that overcame her lack of polish. After a time, Lucy got up the courage to go out on her first auditions. They were primarily for innocuous theater productions and television commercials. Her failure to land anything right away, coupled with the pressures of motherhood, would occasionally weigh on her normally buoyant spirit. Garth would be of help in cheering her up, and, when all else failed, she could always count on her mother's shoulder to cry on. Literally.

"I do remember a time when she was crying on my shoulder," said Julie Ryan of one of her daughter's most discouraged moments. "She was saying, 'I've tried so hard and I can't seem to get a break.' It was very tough for her to get work in New Zealand productions. It's a very closed community and the

casting people seem to have a set group of people
they use all the time. Besides, with Lucy's height, she
would need a leading man who was about seven feet
tall.''

Apart from the upheavals of her incipient career,
Lucy turned twenty happily ensconced in motherhood
and family life. While professional pickings continued to be nonexistent, she was regularly out and about
with Daisy in tow, her ego easily boosted by comments from passersby and neighbors, who noted that
as a mother she was never far from the needs of her
year-old daughter. In fact, she was so devoted to
Daisy that neighbors openly assumed that more children would certainly follow and that Lucy's acting
career would be nothing more than a short-lived lark.
Lucy, of course, felt differently. More children, at
least in the short term, were out of the question; Garth
was in agreement with her on this point. Acting, on
the other hand, was still very much her passion.

Lucy had an early brush with show business and
celebrity in early 1989 when, as a lark, she entered a
beauty contest at the local Tamaki Yacht Club. She
came away with the title of Mrs. New Zealand and
an all-expenses-paid trip for Garth and her to Las Vegas for the Mrs. World finals.

''I had nothing to wear,'' Lawless laughingly recalls, ''so my mother got busy and was literally sew-
ing something together for me as we drove out to the
airport.''

Garth and Lucy spent a week in Vegas at the famed
Flamingo Hotel. Lucy strutted her stuff in the sparkling blue number her mother had cobbled together.

Unfortunately she returned to Auckland without the coveted world crown.

Funny Business was about the hottest thing on the New Zealand comic scene in 1989. Formed in the early eighties by local lads Willy de Wit, Dean Butler, Ian Harcourt, and Peter Murphy, the group's zealous observational brand of humor was an immediate hit on the normally staid New Zealand comedy club circuit. "We were going down quite well in the clubs," recalls de Wit of the time when little money and high energy were the order of the day. "Television seemed the next logical step and so, in 1985, we made a pilot for Television New Zealand that went absolutely nowhere. But, a few years later, that pilot tape was seen by a producer-director named Tony Holden, who took it to television once again and, this time, the powers that be said, 'Okay. Let's make a six-episode series out of this.'"

The first series, heavy on sketch comedy and stand-up routines and beefed up by the addition of a couple of women performers, aired in 1989 and resulted in numerous writing and directing awards for the group. Funny Business was rewarded with a second season of thirteen episodes. Group member Dean Butler recollects that "about that time, the ladies who had been in the group during the first six episodes had decided to go off and do other things. So we had to recast for a couple of female additions to the group."

The core players of Funny Business solicited and received more than fifty audition tapes from aspiring comedians. Holden remembers Lawless's tape as a series of audition-type scenes and sketches from her past auditions, and Butler, while his memory has dimmed on exactly what he saw on Lawless's tape, laughingly remembers "that it was something that definitely struck our fancy. We all looked at it and could tell immediately that she had something special."

"She did not have the background we would normally look for," adds de Wit. "She had no comedy background, no television background, and she had never really done any acting to speak of. We definitely looked at people that were more experienced."

But de Wit also remembers that Lawless, on tape, had an ace up her sleeve.

"Lucy was an incredibly natural person. You could see in her a real sense of ambition and determination. There was just something about her that we just felt we had to use her."

Holden believed he had a handle on what that "something" was. "It was a combination of things physical and internal. She had this fantastic American accent which, for a New Zealand actress, is a miracle. Lucy was tall and stunning and had this ability to change her appearance, which is a real plus in sketch comedy. But I believe what really sold us on her was that she had guts, balls, and determination. You could see that she desperately wanted to be an actor."

Shortly after viewing the tape, the Funny Business crew arranged a meeting with Lawless at their Auckland rehearsal hall. "We all sort of met just to see if we could all get on. Lucy was extremely friendly and outgoing right from the start. Nobody saw any personality clashes in our future in that first meeting.

Then we ran through a couple of sketches with her just to see what she could do.''

During the audition proper, Lawless was tested in such comic elements as comedic timing, delivery, and the ability to handle different characters. ''I could tell that she was nervous during the audition but it seemed that the nervous energy had transformed itself into a very confident persona,'' recalled de Wit. ''She just sort of flew through it all and she handled it all quite well.''

Butler's impression of Lawless's first ever pass at Funny Business schtick was equally positive. ''What we saw in the audition tape and what turned out to be the case when we met was that she was very adept at many different styles of comedy. She had good timing, which can be crucial in comedy routines, and her natural instincts for what to do with a character and a script were very good. We did not need to tell her much about what to do and, when we did tell her something, she was very good about taking direction.''

Shortly after the audition, Lawless signed on as the official new member of Funny Business. The group immediately ensconced themselves in a cavernous rehearsal hall where they spent the next few weeks hammering out the scripts and story lines for the thirteen episodes of Funny Business's second season. A typical Funny Business routine was created in a group session, and then it was run past the show's director to determine what would and would not work before commencing with rehearsals and finally the actual filming of the show.

Lawless was rarely around during that element of the creative process and, according to Butler, "would come in as needed and then we'd just run it." But, far from being a wallflower or a hired hand, de Wit recalls that Lawless immediately had an impact on the group's creative process.

"We could tell right away that Lucy was big on confidence and attitude. She was right there with her input into scripts and story lines. It was typical for her to break into a story conference with 'Could we try it this way?' or 'Could we do it that way?' It was a definite plus to have somebody new tossing about ideas and giving us feedback. Nobody resented it. In fact we welcomed it."

"We definitely saw a difference in Lucy," adds Butler. "A lot of people would have just read the script and done it that way. But Lucy was always looking for ways to improve things. I don't think we expected that from Lucy. But while her willingness to get involved was unexpected, she was offering up a lot of good ideas and we would often end up going with her suggestions."

Because of the low-key nature of Funny Business, nobody blinked an eye when Lawless, on the days when she could not find a baby-sitter or Garth was working, would bring one-year-old Daisy down to the set. "She would regularly divide her time between reading a script, learning her lines, and taking care of Daisy," laughs de Wit. "It all worked out fine and, as a matter of fact, we even ended up using Daisy in a couple of the sketches (one an incredibly funny take on super glue for babies) during the season."

When Funny Business went before the cameras in 1990, Lawless was caught up in the group's unique brand of frenzied energy. She would literally go from one character to another and sometimes play as many as three or four different roles in a typical day of shooting. One day it was the role of a ridiculous entertainment reporter in a hilarious takeoff on shows like *Entertainment Tonight*. Another episode found her dressing down to hilariously repulsive effect in the role of an ugly, abject housewife. De Wit and Lawless once teamed up as a singing duo, à la Sonny & Cher, that belted out bad, schmaltzy songs. In yet another she played the wife of a tow truck driver. And through this trial by comedic fire, Lawless proved herself more than up to the task.

"She just had this natural ability to get stronger and stronger as a performer," says de Wit of Lawless's progress. "There was just this something about her and the camera; it was her strength and it was a quite natural ability. The more she did on camera, the better she got."

As Lawless began to grow in her professional life, Garth continued to be her rock; apparently, he had put any trepidation of what impact her sudden stardom would have on their relationship aside and, according to those in and around Funny Business, presented a picture of total love and support.

"Garth even wound up being in a couple of our sketches as an extra," chuckles Butler. "We all got on pretty well and he seemed to already pretty much have an idea of where Lucy and her career were going and was, to my knowledge, comfortable with that. I know, at the time, they were not making a lot of money and were just getting by but they were quite happily married at that point.''

Holden echoes that opinion of the couple's personal and financial state, citing Garth's constant support for her career. ''Which was wonderful because none of us was making much money at that time. Funny Business was basically a labor of love for us. Lucy was barely making above the level of the dole. Money was tight for Lucy and her husband but that never stopped him from encouraging her and being supportive.''

''You could see that Garth and Lucy had this amazing rapport with each other,'' says de Wit. ''They were very affectionate toward each other and very immersed in Daisy. They were at a very supportive stage with each other at that point.

''I didn't see any discomfort on Garth's part in what Lucy was doing,'' he continues. ''He understood that it was her first big break and that it was providing extra income for the family. I would guess that any problems started happening later when the other things started happening for her. But, at that stage, he was totally supportive.''

This was due no doubt to the fact that, while Lawless could be counted on to be the social butterfly while working, she had not let stardom go to her head. ''Hanging out and hanging around just wasn't Lucy,'' relates de Wit. ''When she was finished working, she tended to go straight home and to keep pretty much to herself.''

As the season continued, the members of Funny

Business were constantly amazed at the ease with which Lawless exchanged comic roles. Punch lines snapped out of her with the crispness of a snare drum rim shot. Lawless had come so far so fast that, by the time Funny Business wrapped its final episode in 1991, the outlook for Lawless remaining with Funny Business if the show was picked up for a third season appeared bleak.

"There was no doubt in my mind that, if we carried on, we wouldn't have Lucy much longer," concedes de Wit. "She was learning and she was getting stronger and stronger as a performer."

Funny Business came to an end shortly after the taping of the thirteenth and final episode was completed when, owing to the insanity of television, those in charge put the completed package in limbo. It would be a year before Lucy's first substantial body of work would air. "We were not sure what was going to happen so we all just decided to pack it in and carry on with individual things," says de Wit. "Lucy leaving Funny Business was just part of that process and it was totally amicable."

Lawless returned temporarily to the life of wife and mother but still actively pursued any and all work. Lawless and Daisy landed a television commercial as a mother blissfully recommending the attributes of a baby carrier. She followed this shortly thereafter, with a series of television commercials for Auckland Savings Bank; once again she played a mum, this time to a child named Stanley whose future was at the hub of the bank's campaign.

Attewell was still a fairly regular fixture in the

Lawlesses' circle at this time and so he had a front row seat to view the Lawless marriage in action.

"As hectic as things could get for them sometimes, I always felt they were the sort of people who would be in it for the long haul. Garth was supportive of Lucy in whatever she wanted to do. Garth had his work as a bar man, but he always seemed to find time to accommodate Lucy's acting schedules. He would take care of Daisy on those occasions when they could not find a sitter and he was the househusband, looking after Daisy when Lucy was on the set. My impression was that Garth was there above and beyond the call of duty."

Lawless, at this point, was an accomplished comedienne and could have easily continued to ply her trade in the laugh arena. But that wasn't Lawless. She was determined to ultimately present a complete package and so she went in search of some dramatic opportunities.

"After Funny Business, Lucy came to me and said, 'I want to be a serious actress,' " says Holden. "She was insistent that she wanted to learn more skill-oriented acting rather than comedy. She wanted to learn dramatic techniques so that she could do serious and emotional parts rather than to continue to just do comedy and act the goat."

Coincidentally, Holden had recently gone from Funny Business to production and directing duties on a limited, ten-episode sitcom with dramatic overtones, called For the Love of Mike. The show, centered around a romantic triangle, followed a woman who gets pregnant by her boyfriend and returns to the work force. The role that appeared right up Lawless's alley was that of the smart and sassy love interest of the boyfriend who got the woman pregnant.

"I really felt Lucy could do it," states Holden. "But I was not about to just give it to her. I think Lucy knew that [our] having worked together on Funny Business was not going to carry a lot of weight and so she worked really hard and ended up being the best person for the part."

Not long after *For the Love of Mike* had finished its run, Lawless had a shot at her first straight dramatic part when producer Holden, who had subsequently moved on to direct *Marlin Bay*, guided her in the direction of a semiregular role in the show's final season. *Marlin Bay*, a New Zealand–made series, told stories about the lives and loves of the people who ran the fictitious Marlin Bay Casino. In a handful of appearances in that series, Lawless showed some spunk and more than a hint of her ability to handle a more serious role as she played a motorbike-riding younger woman entangled in a midlife crisis relationship with the show's older male lead.

"Lucy was very hot and sexy in that role," recalls Holden of Lawless's six-episode stint on *Marlin Bay*. "She was this feisty action woman who rode this bike and always dressed in leather. But she was getting more out of the role than being the token sex symbol. The story line involved a good, deep, serious relationship. It was her first totally dramatic role and she learned quite a bit."

But Lawless, despite these local successes, continued to chomp at the bit. She was public in her concerns that she was not progressing as a performer and excessive in deprecating her own acting abilities.

"She told me, 'Look, Tony! I realize I've only skimmed the surface here,' " relates Holden, " 'but I want to learn more and more and the only way I can do that is to go to acting school.' I reminded her that in New Zealand we really did not have that many acting schools of note. She said, 'Well, I guess I'm going to have to go overseas.' "

Through casual inquiries and conversations with other actors, Lucy heard about the William B. Davis Center for Actor's Study in Vancouver, Canada. The center, founded by the actor noted for his role as the villainous Cigarette Smoking Man on *The X-Files*, had long had a reputation for turning out actors well versed in voice and movement techniques. Lucy felt that furthering her education in Vancouver was the way to go.

Now all she had to do was break the news to Garth.

Garth's support was beginning to fray around the edges. But there was still enough of it so that he did not put up much of an argument when Lawless enthusiastically began to outline her plans for enrolling long distance and eventually settling in Vancouver in time for the school's fall 1991 session.

"Her wanting to go did not really surprise us," comments Holden. "But the fact that she was actually uprooting her family and going to Canada with very little money had us literally in awe. When Lucy decided she was going to Canada to study, all I could say was wow!"

It went without saying that Daisy would accompany Lawless to Canada. Neither would Garth sit by while his wife and daughter went off on what would amount to a year-long adventure without him. Bar jobs were a dime a dozen. His family was a once-in-a-lifetime situation that he was not about to treat casually.

William Davis was in his office, dealing with some of the more mundane chores involved in running an acting school, when the telephone rang. Davis picked up the phone and a tight smile creased his face. He listened, occasionally spoke, and jotted down some information on a piece of paper. Finally he hung up. Davis's artistic director, Garry Davey, walked into the room moments later. Davis told him he had received another call from Lucy Lawless.

"We were quite puzzled," chuckles Davis at the memory of his early telephone conversations with Lawless. "It was like, 'Who was this person?' She was on the phone constantly to make arrangements. Usually people would write letters if they had any questions or needed information. But she thought nothing of getting on the phone and sorting out what needed to be sorted out."

But while Lawless's calls were a constant source of amusement and a slight annoyance, Davis was quick to pick up on something else. "You had to admire her persistence and assertiveness. The conversations I had with her were all very pleasant but it was evident to me that she knew exactly what she wanted to do and she was going to do whatever was necessary to get it."

The Lawless family arrived in Vancouver in early summer of 1991 and settled in a functional apartment in a downtown area called the West End. Shortly thereafter, Lawless decided to get a head start on the fall semester by enrolling in some preliminary scene study, voice training, and general acting technique summer courses at the school. Which is where Davis and Davey finally put a face to the voice on the telephone.

"She struggled like most student actors do," recalls Davey. "But she struggled in a way. . . . She would get upset, stomp her feet, and be real big in her responses. I could see from the beginning that she was a passionate lady. There was a sense about her of being away from her home country and being into a new phase of life that really excited her and it translated into her work."

Davis, who taught many of those summer classes, knew from the outset that "she was incredibly talented.

"That was clear right from the beginning. She had a striking presence and this pleasant sort of aggressiveness that I'm firmly convinced is a down under trait."

As the summer courses drew to a close, Lawless went ahead and auditioned for the fall semester. Davey, however, recalled that the successful audition was just a formality. "We had already worked with her and we could see where she was at. We could already tell that she had a lot of potential."

A potential that continued to be realized when the William B. Davis Center for Actor's Study class of

1991 moved into its formal fall session. The curriculum facing Lawless was much more complex and diversified, containing movement and voice instruction for film and television, improvisation, and a block of Shakespearean theater instruction. Davis's initial impressions of her strengths were justified as the fall classes commenced.

"What jumped out at me during her months here was that she certainly had quick access to her emotional life," he recalls. "That was a constant source of surprise to the other students. If a character had to come into the room crying, she would go out of the room and come back in crying. Everybody's reaction was, How did she do that? It was amazing that she could pick up just the right emotion real fast."

Artistic director Davey agrees with Davis's assessment.

"She was gutsy, real gutsy. She would take bigger chances than some of the other students. Don't get me wrong, Lucy would struggle. Often during class, we would ask her, 'What are you doing now?' and she would say, 'I don't know.' But she always did things with passion; whether she was doing them right or wrong. We had a saying in class, 'Go big or stay at home.' Lucy never stayed at home."

Once instruction moved into detailed scene study, Lawless' budding talents became more evident. One example typical of her showy style of acting came in her interpretation of Agnes, a girl whose dates are few and far between, in the Langford Wilson play *Ludlow Fair*.

"She has this scene in which she is having this big

fight with her roommate while prepping for a date with the boss's son," relates Davey. "It was very complex. The character has a very bad cold, she's fighting, and she's doing her hair and toenails all at the same time. It required a lot of movement and timing. Lucy really went for it."

But while Lawless's stay in Vancouver was thriving in a creative sense, her relationship with Garth was beginning to show its first real signs of strain. When she was not in class, Lawless was spending her free time either in intensive after-hours study or spending quality time with Daisy. Garth, in a strange land and in the middle of an artistic environment, was emotionally isolated. "It was just not working out for her husband," said a candid Davis. "He was having trouble adjusting. He was not happy."

And Garth's state of mind was not lost on Lawless. As always, she was very sensitive to the relationship she was in and was torn by her desires to continue to pursue her artistic dreams while doing whatever was necessary to keep her marriage together. Eventually Garth's frustration and a bad case of homesickness reached the boiling point and, as their days in Vancouver moved toward Christmas 1991, he left Canada and returned to New Zealand. Lawless was in emotional turmoil.

"For personal reasons, she felt she needed to go back to New Zealand," observed Davis. "Going back there at the time did not seem, career-wise, the best place for her to be."

The more intense portion of class study, including full-blown theatrical productions, was scheduled to commence in January 1992 and run through May 1992 graduation. But, as Christmas approached, Lucy Lawless made a very difficult decision.

"If she had her druthers, she would have stayed in Canada," said Davis of Lawless's decision to go back to New Zealand. "But the family situation was just too important to her. She did not want to go back. But, finally, she did."

FIVE

Lucy Gets Lucky

Lawless and Daisy returned to New Zealand in January 1992. If Lawless was unhappy with having to cut short her acting education, it didn't show. She remained loving and understanding toward Garth. But she also remained equally determined to continue with her acting career.

"By the time I came home from Vancouver in 1992, I felt I had received some very fine training," she recalls. "And I was ready to put it to good use."

Lawless wasted little time in reestablishing contacts in the Auckland acting community, letting anybody who would listen know that she was back and ready to work. But what she continued to discover was that the New Zealand acting community was still pretty much a closed shop. "The producers seemed to always go to the same, established people," she explained during those dry days. "When you had reached a certain point, they were all over you. But, when you're on the way up, they can't be bothered."

Consequently when the locally produced travel show, *Air New Zealand Holiday*, approached Lawless to cohost, she jumped at the chance to be in front of the camera again; even if it was simply to hold a microphone and point out the sights of various glamorous hot spots. Hosting the show, which was broadcast throughout New Zealand and Asia, had its perks. Lawless was traveling all over the world. She had a weekly paycheck coming in. She was keeping her face in front of the crowd. And most importantly, in terms of her long-range career aspirations, there was enough significant downtime to allow her to squeeze in some acting jobs as they became available.

One of the first dramatic challenges she encountered upon her return to Auckland was a guest shot in an episode of the syndicated series *The Ray Bradbury Theater*, entitled "Fee Fie Foe Fum." The series was in its final year of production and, to cut financial costs, fifteen of the final twenty-three episodes were being shot in Auckland.

"Fee Fie Foe Fum," which featured respected American actress Jean Stapleton and veteran Canadian actor Robert Morelli, had Lawless playing a disgruntled housewife who is married to a man who is in love with his garbage disposal. So much in love, in fact, that when the housewife's mother's pets begin to disappear under mysterious circumstances, all signs point to something undoubtedly hideous. In the end, the husband and wife live happily ever after. And alone.

Mary Kahn, who produced the episode, recalls that casting primarily New Zealand actors in the secondary roles presented certain challenges that ultimately played to Lawless's acting strengths.

"It's a big struggle in New Zealand to find actors who can do North American accents. Usually what we get when we ask for a North American accent is Texan. Consequently most of the actors cast locally were getting only two or three lines because you couldn't get more than that out of them before their accents started to show."

But Kahn had been hearing through the acting grapevine that Lawless was the exception to the rule. "A lot of actors I had worked with in previous episodes of the show were telling me about her and that she was right for the part of the housewife in 'Fee Fie Foe Fum.' "

The advance word of mouth was confirmed when Lawless auditioned for the role. "I don't think there was any question that she was the appropriate person," says the producer. "We were looking for an actress from New Zealand who had a specific North American look about her. If she had looked the part, we would have been quite happy. But Lucy walked in, looked North American, spoke with a real North American accent, and was a real good actress. Our reaction was, 'Holy cow!' "

Kahn concedes that *The Ray Bradbury Theater* episodes featured the American and Canadian actors and relegated the New Zealand thespians to secondary roles. So Lawless's role, while professionally acted, was not the centerpiece of the story.

John Reid, the director of "Fee Fie Foe Fum," was aware of Lawless's reputation prior to her being cast in the role. He felt going in that, without much dramatic or television experience in her background, the very inexperienced Lawless "was being tossed in the deep end." And he was concerned that Lawless, contrary to producer Kahn's perception, would be playing the pivotal role in the story.

"In the story she played the intermediary between two very strong personalities," he contends. "The relationship, in particular, was pretty claustrophobic, which meant she was going to have the most work to do. From a purely technical point of view, it was very much on Lucy to make the plot work."

Kahn describes Lawless as a total professional. "She learned her lines rather quickly during rehearsals, she was on time, she hit her marks, and she did exactly what was needed for the part. You can't ask for more than that."

Reid, digging into his memory for on-set anecdotes, echoes the at-large perspective of Lawless as "a determined actress who was not afraid of hard work.

"Lucy is a very deceptive personality. She's very tall and very pretty. You don't expect someone as pretty as she is to be so hardworking and determined."

How determined she was came shining through in "Fee Fie Foe Fum" during a sequence when her emotional mettle was truly challenged. "The character she was playing had a huge emotional range to her and the thing that surprised me about Lucy was that she caught onto that emotional range real quickly. There was one scene that called for her to get genuinely upset. One moment Lucy was quite upbeat and joking with people. Suddenly the camera rolled and she literally fell apart right in front of our eyes. She was so genuinely upset that she literally stopped the crew in their tracks.''

That same year, Lawless did a guest shot in the New Zealand–based series *The New Adventures of the Black Stallion*, in the episode entitled ''Riding the Volcano.'' In her scenes, Lawless got to show off a bit more of her physical prowess as a horse trainer who, in the process of breaking a horse, learns that the best way to train a horse is with love and not the whip. Emotionally, Lawless gets to step out in the episode when she is faced with the prospect of having to sell the horse she has finally trained.

Lawless, while continuing to balance family life with the often outrageous demands of *Air New Zealand Holiday*, was more than willing to push her own acting envelope when offered what she considered the right project. Her first movie role, the 1992 short film *Peach*, was just such an opportunity.

Peach, a sixteen-minute short film that is currently being marketed as part of a video collection entitled *Women from Down Under*, is a lesbian film, pure and simple. In it Lawless plays a mysterious tow truck driver who seduces a young mom and encourages her to explore her feelings toward other women. The showstopper in the film has Lawless and the other actress engaging in a hungry kiss.

That same year, Lawless also made her first full-length movie appearance, in the action-adventure film *Rainbow Warrior* (aka *The Sinking of The Rainbow Warrior*). *Rainbow Warrior*, an Auckland-made movie for television, tells the true story of Greenpeace's ship, *The Rainbow Warrior*, which removed from an island people who had been poisoned by atomic bomb experiments and which was sunk by the French Secret Service. Appearing alongside top-lined stars Sam Neill and Jon Voight were a number of local actors, among them Lucy Lawless, portraying a deckhand named Jane Redmond.

Lawless's longtime friend Wakka Attewell, now a full-fledged producer and cinematographer, handled the latter chores on *Rainbow Warrior*. He recalls that while Lawless's role was part of a rather large ensemble cast, she did have her moments.

"Lucy's character was one of reason," he critiques. "When other characters were going to one extreme or another she could be counted on to be right there in the middle. It was not an overly physical role for her. It was very much an acting role and she had lots of dramatic lines."

Attewell also remembers that Lawless, by that time, was beginning to get a reputation among the very small New Zealand acting community. "The consensus was that she had something special. She was already being thought of as one of those great New Zealand actors who was always going to be destined for bigger things."

Lawless's *Air New Zealand Holiday* hosting duties were picked up for a second season in 1993. But while things were going well professionally there was trouble in the Lawless household. Garth, feeling at least subconsciously that he was losing his wife to acting, had begun to become sullen and withdrawn, complaining about her long hours away from home. Lawless, whose attention to family continued to run neck and neck with her career ambitions, did not see it. If anything, her devotion to family seemed to get stronger. During a rather hectic string of days on *Air New Zealand Holiday*, she stated, "If my acting career stopped tomorrow, I'd be alright because I have Garth, my daughter, Daisy, and a wonderful family."

But the image of hearth and home could only go so far in soothing the uneasiness, as Lawless began to feel that her TV hosting chores were not what she had had in mind when she got into acting.

"The show paid okay," recalls Lawless of the source of her growing dissatisfaction. "It was fun and it took me to some thrilling locations. It was also hard work and it was quite uncomfortable at times, and occasionally I'd end up in some country with some godawful Nazi of a guide. But, finally, it was a situation where I really could not tell the whole truth. Some days I would be someplace and I would really want to say, 'Don't come here, this place is crappy.' I knew in my heart that hosting this show was not what I was meant to do. I felt I had reached a crossroads in my life. I felt I could either stay with the show and resign myself to being a big fish in a small pond or risk everything to get what I really felt in my heart I wanted. So I gave up the show even though there was nothing in sight.''

And, coincidentally, Lawless's decision to leave *Air New Zealand Holiday* came just as she entered one of those dry periods where roles were few and far between. She went on a lot of auditions where ''I was just not the type they were looking for'' and just as many where that old bugaboo, her height, worked against her. Lawless, looking back on that dry period years later, had another theory.

''The work I was getting in those early days as an actress always seemed to be either U.S.– or Canadian–New Zealand productions. I always got those jobs but never the strictly New Zealand ones and I truly believe that a lot of that had to do with the fact that I didn't look or act strictly New Zealand. The way I behave can be a little scary to casting people. I think I've always been a little too big for my boots and that probably came across in a lot of those early auditions. My agent was once told by a casting agent for a New Zealand series called *Shortland Street* that 'Lucy doesn't sufficiently fit within the parameters of the show.' I think she was probably quite right. Given my attitude, even if I had gotten the role, I probably would have gotten bored real quickly.''

So it was that 1993 very quickly turned into 1994 with no prospects in sight. But, rather than wilt under the constant barrage of rejection, Lawless's resolve became even more pronounced. ''As an actress, you have to face rejection all the time. Facing rejection made me a real fighter. I kept going up for auditions and, many times, I lost out. But I didn't give up.''

Things finally began to turn around in '94 as Lawless landed a couple of guest shots in the "cops on the high seas" television series, *High Tide*. In the episode "Shanghai," she essayed the role of an undercover policewoman. In the episode "Dead in the Water," she switched sides, playing a woman of questionable motives.

The big news along the Auckland acting grapevine was that *Hercules: The Legendary Journeys* was coming to town. The brainchild of producer and fantasy filmmakers Rob Tapert and Sam Raimi, *Hercules*, a projected series of five two-hour movies for syndicated television on a worldwide scale promised work for local talent on both sides of the camera. For Lucy Lawless the hope was that the wide array of bigger-than-life characters would provide some opportunity for her to showcase her talents. Her prayers were answered, though not quite as she had intended, when she was cast in the role of renegade Amazon Lysia in the movie *Hercules and the Amazon Women*.

But this time, as producer Tapert recalls, word of mouth did not precede Lawless into the *Hercules* audition. Nor did news of her previous limited roles. It all adds up to the fact that Lawless did not get the *Hercules* role she auditioned for.

"When we did the local casting for *Hercules and the Amazon Women*, Lucy initially tested for the lead as the head of the Amazons. And she did quite well in the audition. But, in the end, the studio and the producers simply got cold feet about casting the lead role out of New Zealand. So we ended up casting an actress from Ireland and then had the added expense of flying her down to New Zealand. But Lucy was so good, we ultimately cast her as the badass lieutenant."

Lawless's first appearance in the world of Hercules was a distracting time for the star of the film, Kevin Sorbo. He was just coming to know the rhythm of television movies and the intricacies of special effects and so could hardly be held accountable for remembering the particulars of her appearance. But, after the fact, Sorbo did remember that the young actress seemed very natural as both an actress and an athlete and seemed more than capable of handling the role.

Hercules and the Amazon Women proved a step up for Lawless, with its swordplay, horseplay, and all manner of rough-and-tumble mythological action. It would also be a true test for later roles because, as Lawless readily admits, "my fighting skills were only passable at best." The film's story line follows Lysia, the lieutenant to the Amazon queen Hippolyta, as she created villainous havoc in the life of Hercules while managing to have a carnal relationship with the god Zeus.

"I was sort of the Bolshie lieutenant of the Amazons." Lawless chuckles at the memory of that first encounter with myth and legend. "I brutalized Hercules quite a bit and then we joined forces to rape and pillage a village down the road."

Lawless is a bit shy on particulars when it comes to recalling favorite action sequences in that initial foray into leather costumes and sword fighting. "To be perfectly honest, I don't remember doing those fight scenes. They were all so much of a blur. But I do remember surprising myself by being able to handle the sheer physicality of it all. I felt a natural aggression coming out of me during those scenes that helped me get through it.''

The actress hung up her broadsword at the end of filming and assumed that was that. She felt she had made a proper impression on the producers but she also realized that the odds of her being asked back, even to play the same character, were slim despite the limited New Zealand acting pool.

Lawless was wrong. The producers had been so impressed with her performance in *Hercules and the Amazon Women* that they immediately attempted to go against the prevailing wisdom that warned against casting the same actress in another role on the same show. ''We subsequently attempted to cast her in a lot of different parts in *Hercules*,'' admits Tapert, ''but every time we rang her up, she was off doing something else and was not available.''

But when the package of five *Hercules* movies proved to be a mammoth ratings winner and was converted to a weekly one-hour adventure series in 1995, Lawless not only received a call to come back for the episode entitled ''When Darkness Falls'' but was asked to portray a completely different character, the morally ambiguous Lyla. Lawless was quite happy to return to the series but, she recalls, she did not know why they asked her.

''I don't know why they called me back. I haven't a clue. That's more of a producer's question.''

Indeed. The question was whether producer Rob Tapert had noticed Lawless's acting talents or whether he had found himself smitten with the actress. It was rumored around the *Hercules* set that "Tapert never stopped talking about her" and that every time they were looking for somebody to cast, Tapert would inevitably say, "Let's get Lucy Lawless."

Bruce Campbell, who has known Tapert since before the pair began making waves with the *Evil Dead* movies, says the question of whether Tapert had the warmies for Lawless is "hard to make a judgment on."

"I've only known Rob with one other woman the whole time I've known him," recalls the actor, "and Lucy is nothing like she was. I can only speculate that, if Rob saw anything in Lucy at that point, it was something totally new for him."

Whatever the reason for her being cast, Lawless proved the perfect fit for this latest adventure in the land of Hercules.

"When Darkness Falls" finds Lawless up to her leather tunic in schemes. For openers, Lyla uses her feminine wiles on Hercules and ends up drugging the strongman into submission. And, in conjunction with an equally ambiguous group of centaurs, she goes on to plot further chaos for Hercules to heroically unravel. And, in the capper, Lyla becomes the bride of the centaur Deric. "I was your basic centaur's moll," quips the actress.

Shooting the episode entailed the usual amount of action-adventure sequences and had, as an extra challenge, Lawless playing off special fx-created centaurs that were added in post-production.

"I didn't have any trouble with the special effects," she says. "If you have an active imagination, you just use it and it's not difficult at all. I actually found it easier working off the effects than working off real actors. It never even occurred to me that what I was doing might be difficult. For me, it was just normal acting."

Lawless once again hung up her sword and went home . . . to a family situation that was in tatters. Her upswing in acting roles in '94 and into early '95 was darkly reflected by a downward spiral in her marriage. Garth had become increasingly uncomfortable with her career, and Lawless found her successes tempered by the fact that she and her husband were heading in different directions emotionally.

"I was really surprised when they split up," says Attewell, sighing, of the couple's June 1995 divorce. "I guess you'd have to call it another one of those tragic movie stories. The acting was definitely starting to shift Lucy's head in the short-term if not the long-term. She and Garth just grew further and further apart."

"It was an amicable separation," says Lawless. "Garth and I had just gotten married too young and had just drifted off in different directions."

But while all appeared calm on the surface, Lawless was more than willing to admit that her life was suddenly in turmoil. "Suddenly I was in the middle of a very wild ride. Everything had changed in my life. My marriage had broken up and I was suddenly a single working mother in a highly insecure business.

"At times I felt Daisy did not think that I cared. I

couldn't really defend the decision to split from her father and he had done nothing to justify my speaking ill of him. I felt very much like I was being backed into a corner.''

While Lawless attempted to sort out her personal and professional life, forces were at work behind the scenes that would forever change her life. *Hercules: The Legendary Journeys*, midway through its first full season, was proving to be a surprise of major proportions. Ratings worldwide were way up and the creative minds behind the show were wracking their brains, attempting to come up with story lines that would keep the momentum going. Producer Tapert, long a fan of the female fighting women of the Hong Kong cinema, fashioned the idea of Xena, a tough-as-nails, take-no-prisoners warrior, initially on the side of evil, who, while dealing with Hercules in various adventures over the proposed three-episode arc, has a change of heart and goes over to the side of good.

''I believe there's a formula to stories about heroes,'' says Tapert, explaining his initial conception of Xena. ''No one has ever tried it before with a woman or, if they did, they made excuses for her being a woman. I felt a warrior woman, without the excuses, would work.''

All hands conceded, from the beginning, that Xena would fade into the mists of time at the end of the third episode. ''There was no thought of Xena being anything more than a temporary character,'' relates scriptwriter John Schulian, who wrote two of the three Xena episodes. ''I created Xena with nothing more in mind than getting to the season's end.''

With an eye toward the growing, and quite lucrative, North American market for *Hercules*, the producers and studio executives felt that casting an American actress in the role of Xena was in their best interest. After a protracted casting call Vanessa Angel (who would go on to star in the television series *Weird Science*) was selected for the role of Xena and was put into an accelerated training program to pump her up for the physical demands of playing the part.

Angel was trained by martial arts master Douglas Wong, who also prepped Kevin Sorbo for the rigors of *Hercules*. Wong, in all candor, admits that Angel was not shaping up as a world beater.

"She was not very strong," says Wong. "She was pretty meek and weak at what she was doing and she did not have the confidence to do a lot of the things that I wanted her to do."

Fate stepped in late in 1995, when Angel, at the worst possible moment, reportedly came down with a serious ailment and was not able to fly down to New Zealand to do the role. Wong dispels that rumor by saying the "serious illness" was a smokescreen for a sudden attack of romance.

"The rumor that Vanessa got sick is not true. At the time she went to England and ran with Richard Gere. All of a sudden she lost interest in the part."

When asked about it, producer Tapert chuckled nervously at the suggestion that Vanessa Angel's departure from *Xena* was a matter more of the heart than of illness. "I've heard the story that I owe Richard Gere a thank-you and I'm not going to deny that story has been around. But, I think for insurance purposes, the story should remain that Vanessa Angel had a really bad flu.''

In a panic, producers Tapert and Raimi recalled that Lawless, in the previous *Hercules* outings, had proven a capable actress and more than up to the physical demands. They quickly trotted her name before the studio executives as a last-minute replacement who was only a phone call away. ''We told the studio, 'She's been training for a month,' '' recalls Tapert, '' 'so why don't we just use Lucy Lawless?' ''

''They rejected me at first,'' recalls Lawless with more than a touch of irony in her voice. ''When they heard my name, one studio executive said, 'Are you crazy?' They were insistent that they wanted a new face but that it had to be an American actress. Which, at that time, was all right with me. I wasn't really all that keen on being a female superhero. I needed the work but I still had designs that I would, someday, be this Shakespearean kind of actress.''

The producers were disappointed that Lawless had been cut out of the picture, and Schulian, in particular, was convinced that Lawless was the perfect choice. ''I was very disappointed that Lucy had not been given a shot,'' says Schulian. ''At the time, we were looking at dailies from 'When Darkness Falls' and, as soon as I saw her in the dailies, I said, 'She should have been Xena.' You could see that she was a remarkably good-looking woman.''

Whatever her reservations about the role, Lawless was disappointed. But she put a positive spin on it by using the free time to bundle Daisy off to a less traveled area outside the city for a ''just us girls'' camping experience. She left word and a number with a trusted cousin. The word was "Don't contact me unless it's an emergency or something real important."

In the meantime a short list of American actresses had been cobbled together by the studio heads and the producers were burning up the telephone lines talking to agents in an attempt to get somebody to sign up to play Xena. And they were having no luck.

"It was like, 'Here's a list of five other actresses you should try,' " recalls Lawless, having heard the story secondhand. "And every one of them pulled out for some reason. Pilot season was coming up so they decided, 'Oh, no! We don't want to go down to the bottom of the world in pilot season and do a three-week stint that will come to nothing when we could stay here in L.A. and do a pilot that could possibly become a series.' "

In a last desperate attempt, Tapert and Raimi convinced the Hercules bean counters that Lawless was perfect for the part, "was in country and was available," and that they could get her with a telephone call. Unfortunately, when that call was made, nobody picked up.

And the reason was that Lawless and Daisy were in the middle of what she described as "a podunk town" attempting to have what she hoped would be "a wonderful camping experience" and meeting with less-than-hoped-for success.

"I was fighting the flu," recalls Lawless, "and Daisy and I were literally out in the middle of nowhere. The town was so small that they had shut down the newspaper for three days because there just was not enough news to report. So, to pass some of the time, I would be reading all the horoscopes in back issues. One of mine said, 'Fame and fortune await you.' And, being as sick as I was, all I could think was 'Yeah, sure.' ''

In the meantime, the *Hercules* producers were working overtime to track Lawless down. When numerous calls to Lawless's number went unanswered, they turned detective and began tracking down family members. ''They were moving heaven and earth to find me.'' Lawless chuckles at the memory. ''First they tried my family and they didn't know. Finally the casting agent for the show thought to try my then in-laws and, as it turned out, they knew to try my cousin.''

Lawless was decidedly down in the dumps when she received a telephone message that the producers of *Hercules* needed to talk to her right away. She did not know what to think when she got on the phone with them. When she got off the phone with the knowledge that she would be playing this character Xena, she was in a state of shock.

''All I could think of was to say, God bless those other five actresses who turned the part down,'' she remembers. ''First they didn't want me, then all of a sudden, they wanted me. It was an incredible feat of serendipity.''

Lawless, literally in a daze, gathered up Daisy and their camping gear and got on the first bus going back to Auckland. And as the bus pulled out of the middle of nowhere, heading for Auckland, Lawless instinctively flashed on the fact that Xena might have more in store for her than just three episodes' worth of work.

"Suddenly I just burst into tears. I thought, 'I'm not ready for this.'"

SIX

Xena: Take One

L ucy Lawless sat back in her seat as the plane taxied down the runway in preparation for takeoff
from the Auckland, New Zealand, airport. She closed
her eyes as the plane sped down the tarmac and gradually lifted off. She barely heard the thump as the
landing gear folded up into the belly of the plane.
Lawless took a deep breath and let it out in a sigh.

It was the first time in the last forty-eight hours that
she had the opportunity to relax and she was going
to milk every second. Because she sensed that crazy
days were about to come.

The moment Lawless and Daisy had gotten off the
bus, she was pulled in different directions. She was
formally informed that she had landed the part of
Xena in the three-part *Hercules* arc. Lawless was also
informed that she would have to fly to Los Angeles

in two days to formally accept the role, meet with the stateside producers, and be fitted for a costume and appropriate hairstyle. It went without saying that Daisy would stay with her father, adding credence to the notion that the Garth-Lucy separation had, indeed, been amicable. Then there was a confab with the New Zealand casting director, when Lawless got a preliminary walk through Xena's world and the first script, entitled "The Warrior Princess." Then there was just enough time for a sleepless night, and Lawless was off to the airport.

Lawless's plane touched down at Los Angeles International Airport. From its final approach in to its taxiing up to a smooth stop, her face was glued to the window, taking in the slightly overcast day that was Los Angeles in midautumn. She was fighting jet lag but the sight of a handwritten sign with her name on it, held by a limo driver, immediately jarred her out of her lethargy.

There was a relatively quick ride through notoriously bad Los Angeles traffic, an equally brief stop to check in to a fancy hotel and to freshen up, and finally the beginning of a whirlwind two days in which the nuts and bolts of Xena's physical appearance were tightened into place.

Having already appeared in various forms of wild warrior dress in her previous *Hercules* appearances, Lawless had pretty much expected more of the same when she walked into an elaborate wardrobe department. But even so, she had moments when she giggled as the leather minidress with faux metal trappings and elaborate chain mail bustier were

tucked and fitted into a comfortable, and just revealing enough, costume.

When it came to hair color, however, Lawless had
some concerns. "The original idea they had for Xena
was to make her very blond and very buxom," remembers Lawless, whose true hair color tends to run
to a reddish brown with hints of gold. "The blond
part worried me because I didn't want to deal with
all those chemicals and end up with all my hair falling
out. So I said, 'Why don't we go this way? Let's
make her kind of an Argentinean princess and bronze
her up.' "

That seemed like a good idea to the *Hercules* people. Ultimately a compromise was reached. Lawless
sighed with relief when it was finally determined that
her hair could stay its natural color for her *Hercules*
appearances. Lawless had won the battle of the hair
color but ultimately lost the war of the hair extensions. "Those things are ghastly," she groans. "No
one can run their fingers through my hair."

In the meantime, the *Hercules* writers and producers were putting the final touches onto the three-story
arc and, while not even remotely thinking in terms of
a series at this point, were already making noises in-
dicating that, in the back of their minds, Xena might
just be around for a while.

The Xena origin story, a collaborative concoction
between the producers and writers, with R. J. Stewart
writing the actual script, opens with Xena as a humble
peasant girl. Marauding raiders attack her village and
kill her brother. Since no one else will stand up to the
raiders, Xena begins to learn the art of war. Xena

eventually builds her own army and defeats the raiders. But Xena's lust for revenge does not stop. To make sure no one will ever invade her village again, she sets out to conquer the surrounding lands. Eventually Xena continues to wage war for no other reason than the love of power, causing her name to echo in fear across the civilized world.

"We're giving Xena a kind of steely resolve," says Producer Tapert, hearkening back to Xena's Hong Kong fighting woman influences. "We're also giving Xena a more mature perspective than Hercules. It's pretty basic and easy to understand. With Xena we have a character whose way of carrying herself states, 'I have something to say but I can't quite say it yet.' That idea will deepen before it is ultimately resolved. We immediately saw the theme of Xena as being the story of a hero we hope is within us and something more about the concept of being a hero than Hercules is."

Lawless, upon reading the finished draft of "Hercules and the Warrior Princess" just days before stepping before the camera, already had an idea of what Xena was going to be. "In that first script, Xena was really using her sexuality. You could see that she was very imperialistic in her attitude but, at the core of her being, she was very much the vixen."

Lawless returned to Auckland three days after her trip to Los Angeles and literally had enough time to take Daisy in her arms and run through the finished script one more time . . . before stepping before the cameras for the first time as Xena, on a cool but not cold early morning along the picturesque rolling landscape that served as the place where Hercules plied his adventurous trade.

"The Warrior Princess," which officially kicked off the Xena odyssey, proved a delightfully dark outing. In it, the basic premise of Xena as an evil entity is set up as the warrior princess, at the head of a marauding army whose goal is to hunt down and ultimately kill Hercules, sets a seductive trap for Hercules' best friend Iolaus, driving a seemingly insurmountable wedge between them. "The Warrior Princess" turned out to be a well-crafted episode, balancing the need to keep Hercules very much in the story line while showcasing Xena's abilities as a horsewoman and action star, complete with ringing swordplay and lots of running and jumping.

"It was like everything I had done in my life came into play in that episode," remarks Lawless, looking back on "The Warrior Princess." "All the rough-and-tumble play with my family and the running and jumping I did at play. It was like just about every physical challenge that came up, I could reach into my bag and pull out the appropriate ability."

Which was a happy surprise for those who had gone out on a pretty short limb in insisting that she be cast. Because if there was one question mark regarding Lawless's ability to project a believable Xena, it was the physical aspect. Not that Lawless was not in shape. She was very much the athletic specimen and worked just hard enough to keep herself that way. But with the possibility of a full-blown series looming ever closer, the "Warrior Princess" script seemed to up the ante in terms of action challenges beyond anything that had been asked of her in the two previous *Hercules* movies. The question of whether Lawless was up to the task was answered the first time the producers took a look at the actress in action while viewing dailies.

"When I saw her in the dailies for the "Warrior Princess" episode, and saw the way she rode a horse and swung a sword, I thought, This is money in the bank," relates Schulian. "She was fun to watch and you could tell she wasn't just going through the motions. Lucy was really getting into it."

Lawless was not so convinced. While confident that she was athletic, the actress was having the first of many ongoing doubts about her ability to kick ass in a fantasy environment. "I had been trained and bullied into some level of proficiency," she says, wincing at the memory of her first Xena outings. "But when I started, my coordination was pretty hopeless."

Easily one of the most hilarious moments in "The Warrior Princess," and an early indication of Xena's overt sexuality, took place early one morning in an Auckland warehouse. Lawless and New Zealand actor Michael Hurst (who plays Iolaus) stepped gingerly out of their dressing rooms and walked over to a sunken tub filled nearly to the top with water. There was not much steam rising from the surface, which moved Hurst to test the water temperature by sticking his big toe in. He jumped back and announced to Lawless, his New Zealand sense of humor intact, that the water was no better than lukewarm. And it was under those conditions that the two actors would have to play out the erotic sequence in which Xena disrobes and joins Iolaus in the tub as part of her plan of seduction and betrayal.

Episode director Bruce Seth Green, having completed a conference with his cameraman on the fine art of showing just enough skin but not too much, wandered over to where Lawless and Hurst were standing and dutifully heard their complaints about the water temperature. Making matters worse, it was discovered that Styrofoam bits, used to simulate stone in the tub, were coming loose and turning the tureen into something resembling a tureen of soup. Director Green assured the actors that the scene would only require a couple of takes and then called for action. Hurst eased himself into the tub, making funny faces that immediately reduced the crew to guffaws of laughter. At Green's call to "roll it," Lawless, trying her best to look the evil seductress, climbed into the tub. She looked into Hurst's eyes and they both dissolved into gales of laughter.

Looking back on the sequence, Hurst is at a loss to describe how the scene ever got shot at all. "Needless to say, the last thing on either one of our minds was a sense of eroticism," chuckles the actor. "We tried to be businesslike about it just to get it over with but we could not help but lose it. It was impossible not to laugh at the whole ridiculous situation."

Xena returned to action in the second episode, entitled "The Gauntlet," in which our heroine, having begun to tire of her evil ways, is contemplating leaving that life behind and taking another path, possibly crusading for good. "The Gauntlet" turned out to be a transitional episode in the most extreme sense.

Unlike "The Warrior Princess," "The Gauntlet" immediately introduced dark and hard-edged qualities that seemed intended to make Xena a decidedly separate entity from Hercules. In the episode Xena, at one point, has to decide whether or not to kill a baby. When she declines to do the deed, this random act of kindness puts Xena at odds with her army. When her former followers mutiny in the face of Xena's turn to good, the warrior princess must fight through a gauntlet of her own warriors. "The Gauntlet," although serving as a worthy setup to Xena's conversion to good, still gets mixed reviews.

"I thought 'The Gauntlet' was a little too dark," concedes Schulian. "It was the case of a relatively inexperienced director seeking to make his mark, and what happened was, he made his mark so well that he did not make the show."

Lawless, likewise, had mixed feelings about the episode, admitting that the proceedings were a bit too intense. "But I liked the way it showed Xena's changing character. Before, she had no honor, but this Xena is very different. What happens to her in 'The Gauntlet' is part of a very real life-changing transition."

Lawless's athletic prowess continued to be put to the test. The titanic battle with her own army at the episode's end provided the actress with more than her share of bumps, bruises, and bloody scrapes. But even at that early stage the cast and crew marveled at how quickly Lawless was either bouncing back from or

Lucy Lawless offers a sly grin during her stay in Las Vegas—of course, even Caesar's Palace can't compare to the centaurs and giants of Xena's ancient Greece! *Credit: Gilbert Flores/Celebrity Photo Agency.*

While at a New Orleans convention, Lucy takes a break from all that tiresome leather and steel in favor of this slinky gown, proving that there's more than one way to slay a crowd. *Credit: Janet Gough/Celebrity Photo Agency.*

Lucy, demonstrating the flexible weave of her new dress, at the opening of Universal Studios Florida's latest attraction, "Hercules and Xena, Wizards of the Screen." Kevin Sorbo looks on, apparently outmatched. *Credit: Reuters/Joe Skipper/Archive Photos.*

Nothing like a new sword to put a smile on a girl's face. Lucy cuts up at the opening of "Hercules and Xena, Wizards of the Screen." *Credit: Reuters/ Joe Skipper/ Archive Photos.*

Jay Leno, in a moment of nationally televised abandon, actually puts his hand on Lucy's wrist. Whoa there, fella! Entire civilizations have fallen for less! *Credit: Reuters/Margaret Norton/nbc/Archive Photos.* RIGHT, NEXT PAGE: Finally getting the credit she deserves, Lucy is carried onto the set of *The Tonight Show with Jay Leno* in regal style, following her mishap suffered while practicing a stunt for *The Tonight Show. Credit: Reuters/Margaret Norton/nbc/Archive Photos.*

While accompanying Danny Aiello as he is roasted at the New York Friar's Club, Lucy proves once again that just because she can whip Ares in a fight doesn't mean she can't do a dishy turn in a dress. *Credit: Reuters/Jeff Christensen/Archive Photos.*

Lucy picks Kevin Sorbo's wallet while at a convention. Ha-ha, just kidding. *Credit: Janet Gough/Celebrity Photo Agency.*

Lucy Lawless swats an irksome fly at a New Orleans convention. *Credit: Janet Gough/Celebrity Photo Agency.*

completely ignoring the rough-and-tumble that was a big part of playing Xena.

"I've actually gotten much better at that," reported Lawless shortly after completion of the *Hercules* trilogy. "When the camera rolls, I don't even think about it much anymore. I think my reflexes, after getting hit a few times, have actually gotten quite a bit sharper."

Veteran character actor Robert Trebor, who would go on to play the super salesman Salmoneus in a number of Xena episodes in the *Hercules* series, appeared in the episodes "When Darkness Falls" and "The Gauntlet" opposite Lawless. And the way he remembered the experience in a recent interview, it was love at first sight.

"I found Lucy to be very sexy and very flirtatious. She was fun to be around."

The transition that Xena was making in "The Gauntlet" would soon be mirrored in Lucy Lawless's own life. By this time the episode "The Warrior Princess" had made its way across the world and into the executive screening room at Universal Studios, the distributor of *Hercules*. To say that they were impressed with Lawless's work is an understatement of mammoth proportions. They liked what they saw of this Amazon fighting woman and memos and telephone calls were going back and forth across the world with the same basic theme: that a weekly Xena series would not be such a bad idea.

Tapert's good buddy Bruce Campbell, who was getting from the producer a regular earful on Xena's odyssey, laughs at the notion of the studio executives'

lather over Xena. "The Universal executives saw the
three-episode *Hercules* arc and obviously got a
woodie over Lucy."

But Tapert knew, despite the initial rush of enthusiasm, that the studio heads were proceeding with
caution about greenlighting a weekly Xena series.
"Xena was real risky at that point and was definitely
on the bubble in the minds of the studio executives.
Discussions had reached the point where it depended
on one man to say yes or no and that one person had
not decided yet. And you really could not fault his
indecision because there was not a history of successful female superhero shows on television. The last
female superhero show of any consequence was *Wonder Woman* and that show was not real successful.
Consequently the studios were concerned that young
boys would not watch a female superhero who beat
up guys."

Tapert, who felt that a Xena series would be more
than capable of knocking off the reigning syndication
champ *Baywatch*, felt the studio heads were dead
wrong in their thinking.

"I always felt that *Xena* would be very relevant for
kids and, by association, young guys," he attested.
"Action, monsters, and, if they got it, humor would
definitely work on a male audience. I just wanted to
make the kind of show I would watch, the kind of
show I would have fought with my parents to watch."

The first inkling Lawless had that Xena might
be something more than a one-shot appearance came
during the filming of "The Gauntlet." Lawless, between scenes, was sitting in the assistant director's

bus, having lunch, when producer Tapert appeared and, out of the blue, tossed out the fact that the first Xena appearance was meeting with positive feedback and that the executives were talking about a weekly Xena series. Lawless, already wise to the fact that talk is cheap, took Tapert's comments with a grain of salt.

"I was trying to be real cool about it," laughed Lawless as she remembered the moment. "I said, 'Yeah, yeah, I'll believe it when it happens and I'll talk to you later, Mr. Tapert.' I went off and had lunch on my own and tried to pretend I hadn't heard what I heard."

Lawless did talk to Tapert later. In fact, by that time, a budding and largely secret romance between Lawless and the producer was well in bloom. In a sense, it was not surprising. Since *Hercules* had gone from its series of two-hour movies to its weekly one-hour status, Tapert had been spending an increasing amount of time in New Zealand. And, consequently, more time around Lawless during her early Xena appearances. Tapert had also recently ended a twelve-year relationship with screenwriter Jane Goe and, like Lawless with her equally recent separation, was suffering the pangs of loneliness.

According to observers, the relationship started out as a strictly professional one, taking the form of good-natured conversations and barbs tossed back and forth on the set. But even at that point one could see the first signs of chemistry. Tapert, all business but with a devilish sense of humor and style beneath the veneer, mixed well with Lawless's enticing blend of naïveté and a natural, outgoing personality. Eventually

Tapert's stays in New Zealand became even longer
as preparation for the Xena trilogy proceeded, and the
behind-the-scenes conviction that Xena would go
weekly became stronger.

"The kind of thing that happened between Rob and
Lucy is such a kooky thing," offers Campbell.
"They're both so intimate with the show on a professional level. I have no idea how something like
that becomes personal but, in their case, it just did."

By November 1995 the pair was deeply in love and
deeply involved. But Lawless, still attempting to deal
with single motherhood, was cautious. "He's [Tapert]
the finest man I've ever met and I consider myself a
very lucky person," said Lawless not too long after
the relationship blossomed. "I'm only seeing him
about once a month right now and we have no inten-
tion of living together. At this point all I can say is
we'll see how it works out."

For the time being, however, love and romance
were taking a backseat to filming the third element of
the Xena arc, "Unchained Heart." In this episode we
get a surprisingly detailed look into the psyche of
Xena as she makes the decision, in agonizingly hes-
itant steps, to leave her evil past behind and attempt
to remake herself in the heroic mold.

"Unchained Heart" proved to be Lawless's tough-
est acting challenge to date. Xena's transformation
had to be done in tightly honed stages. Too much
good too fast would have knocked the original concept of redemption into a cocked hat. And it is to
Lawless's credit that Xena comes across as nothing

if not tortured as she attempts to come to terms with her past and make amends for it.

Lawless proved very adept at anguish and pathos and, while the thrust of "Unchained Heart" was still action and swordplay, with a mere turn of her head or a suddenly icy stare she was able to cast more than enough doubt that Xena, though on the path of goodness, would never be totally free of the rage that simmered inside her. And it was Lawless's acting in "Unchained Heart," speculates co–executive producer and writer R. J. Stewart, that cinched Xena making the jump to a weekly series.

"She does the action so convincingly and she is obviously very beautiful," he asserts. "But, even though you may like an actor, you never really know until you see your words being said by them. Lucy knew the part inside and out. She was believable in all aspects of the role."

While Lawless was drawing raves from the front lines, Tapert and Raimi were dealing with studio executives who, while high on Xena, were dealing from an old deck of television standards. There were memos regarding the costume and how revealing it would be. How much violence would be involved and how graphic would it be? Would Xena have sex? Would Xena have a boyfriend? Tapert, with one hand firmly on the Xena bible and both feet planted firmly on his principles, was determined to do Xena his way.

"A boyfriend for Xena? That will never happen," says the producer, chuckling as he recalls those meetings and memos. "There would be romance but we planned on making it very plain that she had had a string of lovers in her life and, while she would occasionally take a lover, she was just trying to get ahold of her emotions. The studio also said, 'Can you get her to turn around so that she is suddenly totally good?' I said, 'I guess I could but it would not be as much fun.' "

By December 1995, word officially came down that *Xena: Warrior Princess* had been given the green light as a weekly one-hour show. Everyone connected with the show was ecstatic.

"I did not believe what I was hearing," Lawless relates of the day she heard the news. "I did not expect anything like *Xena* to happen for at least another five years. I was thoroughly convinced that I would have to go to the States and break in there. And, all of a sudden, it was happening as far away from Hollywood as one could possibly get. It came at just the right time. I was trying to figure out how I was going to manage to support Daisy and myself on my own. I figured after the three episodes of Xena, I would have to start worrying about it again.

"Suddenly I had nothing to worry about."

SEVEN

Physical Education

It seemed like every time Lawless turned around, she was on a plane heading for Los Angeles. This time, following a relatively sedate New Year's Eve spent with, at turns, Daisy and Rob, she was leaving Auckland for a four-week crash course in being an effective Xena. It was not going to be like the last trip to L.A. It was going to take more than a costume fitting, hair extensions, and a hair-color change to make things right.

Xena: Warrior Princess was now a weekly series and that meant a lot more work. Lawless, in the ensuing four weeks, would learn the art of acting for the camera, brush up on dialogue and movement techniques, and, easily the most important, learn the variety of fighting moves and weapons techniques required of a full-time warrior princess.

Once again Douglas Wong, at Tapert's request, was pressed into service to create the ultimate fighting woman. And Tapert's instructions, recalls Wong, were literally to do the impossible.

"Rob showed me a video of one of the women fighters from a Hong Kong action movie. It contained moves like jumping heel kicks, kicks to the neck, and, basically, a whole bunch of impossible things. I told Rob, 'Well, we can get something going but I don't think we can get anything like that.' I told him, 'You're not giving me enough time to work with her. A person with ten years' experience would not be able to do that stuff.' He said, 'Well, work with her and see what you can do.' I said, 'Okay. No problem.' "

Wong's approach to turning actors into super fighters is first to determine what kind of athlete they are and what they are capable of doing. One look at Lawless's appearances in the *Hercules* movies and episodes was enough to convince the martial arts instructor that, physically, she was already in the ballpark.

"I saw that she was capable of doing some basic martial arts–type moves. At that point she was okay; she did not look too bad at all. The stunt coordinator on the show had trained her to do the movements well enough. But I could also tell that she did not understand the techniques behind the movements."

Lawless was upbeat but cautious when she walked into Wong's studio that first day. "I had never thought of myself as a real physical person," she recalls of those first-day jitters. "I knew I was not a natural sportsman like Kevin Sorbo. I knew I needed to get my skills up and keep them up because the physical stuff does not come naturally to me.''

Wong readily put Lawless at ease and, after about five minutes of casual conversation during which time he gauged her athletic ability, ''we just got down on the floor and did it.''

But not without some stumbling starts. As with every new experience in her life, Lawless charged right in and immediately found herself in over her head. ''She was frustrating herself the first couple of days of training,'' remembers Wong of those early days of intense flexibility exercises and short stick and staff work. ''Lucy was having trouble remembering the movements. But by the third day she was very much on it. I could tell right away that Lucy was very strong-minded. She kept telling herself she was going to master these skills and she did.''

Under Wong's guidance, Lawless soon mastered the flexibility exercises that would allow her to do dramatic and lethal high kicks. Her work with the staff—in particular, the trademark figure-eight movements—were her first step toward performing intricate maneuvers with her broadsword. Lawless was also quick to pick up on the basic kung fu moves that would be necessary in combating mythological evil. Time was also spent teaching Lawless both offensive and defensive rolls and falls.

''There was nothing modern-day in the fighting approach I was teaching Lucy,'' explains Wong. ''Because of the nature of the show, Lucy was being taught to fight on walls and on horseback. It was pretty much an old style of fighting. But she picked it up very quickly and, by the end of four weeks, she was just smoking on it.''

When Lawless was not learning fighting skills, she was going toe to toe with acting teachers and dialogue coaches in marathon sessions designed to get the young actress comfortable with her new role as a series star who would be in front of the camera longer than she had ever been before. Once again it was a struggle, but Lawless was nothing if not enthusiastic about this crash course.

''It felt like the old studio system,'' she laughs. ''They had whisked me off to Los Angeles and were teaching me all kinds of things. The experience was just wonderful and it really kick started me again.''

Lawless returned to Auckland in late January and immediately settled into what would be an endless cycle of sixteen-hour days, beginning with the inaugural episode of *Xena: Warrior Princess*, entitled ''Sins of the Past.'' This episode does not waste any time in establishing Xena as a somewhat reformed but still conflict-ridden individual.

In ''Sins Of The Past,'' Xena attempts to reestablish her life in her hometown of Amphipolous. But, early on, in a scene in which Xena wavers on whether to give a young orphan a morsel of food, we know that the warlord has not completely changed her spots. The struggles continue when Xena arrives home and the villagers and even her mother doubt the sincerity of her new life. Along the way Xena's warrior ways once again surface when she wades into a group of mercenaries who are rounding up women for not-so-nice purposes and, in a rapid-fire series of swordplay and martial arts sequences that incorporate much of what Wong had taught her weeks earlier, she dispatches them in now-vintage Xena fury.

According to producer Stewart, "the reformed Xena has not lost her fighting edge and there is a certain dark tone to the series. At the beginning of the pilot Xena is burying her weapons; it's a symbol that she's turning away from her past life of violence. But, as we see in 'Sins of the Past,' Xena cannot leave her past completely behind."

Shooting in and around Auckland, *Xena*'s production schedule very quickly became a victim of the wildly unpredictable weather. How tough it could be on Lawless, who was just getting used to television production as a nonstop run on a circular wheel, became painfully evident while shooting the second episode, "Chariots of War." As the title suggests, Xena spends much of that episode racing in chariots over hills and across sandy beaches. What Lawless had not counted on was their filming right in the middle of one of the worst winters on record. *Xena* editor Robert Field recalls painfully watching the endless takes of Lawless on his editing machine and feeling a lot of sympathy for the young actress. "She was wet and cold, in and out of that chariot and freezing her ass off."

"It was bitter cold," Lawless recalls with a wince. "I was wearing wet leather and it was sleeting and we were driving chariots right into the teeth of the wind. I would cower down inside the chariot in between takes and keep saying to myself, 'This too shall pass.' ''

Nonetheless, Lawless's willingness to try anything remained undiminished and came into play during the inaugural season's fourth episode, "Cradle of Hope."

"I remember reading the script," relates "Cradle of Hope" director Michael Levine, "and I came upon this scene that said Xena breathes fire. I said, 'How is Lucy going to do that?' ''

Lawless, not surprisingly, was game and after a conference that included stunt personnel, Lawless, and Levine, she was instructed on the process of putting the flammable liquid in her mouth and spitting it out on cue. On the day the scene was to be shot, the assembled cast and crew were cautiously optimistic. Levine finally called for action and Lawless spat out flames. "She really did it herself," remembers Levine with obvious relish. "There was no stunt person or computer enhancement involved. It was all Lucy."

In "Cradle of Hope" Lawless also executed an intricate dance sequence that produced some hilarious outtakes but a competent finished product and was part of the show-stopping fight sequence with baby toss. Lawless executed the sequence—toss the baby, fight, catch the baby, and toss it again—with a full array of sword moves and expressive looks and, at one point, took on the role of cameraperson as she held the camera under one arm and moved it back and forth to simulate the baby's point of view.

Lawless and *Hercules* star Kevin Sorbo had gotten friendly during her first appearances in *Hercules: The Legendary Journeys* but, once *Xena* went to series, their long hours and crazy schedules kept the pair from getting together to compare notes on each other's experiences. The pair did find some time shortly after the first season of *Xena* began, and Sorbo remembers their conversation centered on luck and timing.

"We talked about how lucky an actor is to get a series and how, if it becomes a hit, it's a matter of incredible luck and good fortune. I told her there were probably ten thousand actresses in Los Angeles who wanted to kill her because she didn't go through years of paying her dues before getting her big break. I also told her that she was Xena."

While still new to the character, Lawless, likewise, was quick to pick up on the fact that a flawed character was an interesting character. "The only way Xena is going to work is to keep her a redeemed character or a character struggling with her redemption. If she had come from *Hercules* and suddenly become this wholesome do-gooder, there would not be a whole lot to keep an audience tuning in.

"Xena is a character who survives in a strange, dangerous world because she knows everything about the dark side of human nature," she continues. "She used to be bad herself and she uses that. But she's not the totally reprehensible woman she was in *Hercules*. She's learned some things about herself and so she's a lot less nasty."

But even an enticingly flawed character has the potential of getting old if always alone, which is why the writers, in their wisdom, chose to have Xena, during the first episode, hook up with the wholesome,

Greek myth–spouting Gabrielle (actress Renee
O'Connor). A positive counter to Xena's negative
tendencies, Gabrielle's a sidekick whose sheer mo-
rality and goodness make her the perfect foil and confidant for Xena.

O'Connor met Lawless in Los Angeles while au-
ditioning for the part of Gabrielle and the two immediately struck up a friendship. "Lucy had such an
amazing sense of humor," recalls the actress of her
first meeting with Lawless. When O'Connor did land
the role of Gabrielle and relocated to New Zealand,
Lawless met her at the airport, ready and willing to
continue the relationship and help the young actress
settle into the New Zealand way of life.

The grind that is weekly television continued as
Xena: Warrior Princess plunged headlong into its inaugural season. The episode "Dreamworker," which
has the requisite sword and action scenes, also constituted a new acting challenge for Lawless. In the
story, Xena comes face to face with the ghosts of
villagers she has killed in her former dark life and
battles the repressed excitement that blood lust brings.
There was much going on in this episode, and Lawless's ability to make it all believable finally dispelled
any lingering doubts that this leggy actress could really act.

Lawless, while regularly putting in sixteen-hour
days on the set, was also managing to keep her domestic side fairly intact. Her split with Garth had been
so amicable that her former husband had no problem
agreeing to help her out by taking care of the now

seven-year-old Daisy when the child was not in school.

"It's difficult sometimes but we're managing," remarks Lawless of the admittedly out of kilter family relationship. "Daisy comes down to the set after school some days and, when she does not, I know she's well looked after because she's with her father. And, in my opinion, she couldn't have a better father so I know she's fine."

At that point, Daisy had only seen Xena appear in the *Hercules* episodes. According to Lawless, "She thinks it's pretty cool. But she hasn't seen any of the new *Xena* episodes yet so I guess it's hard to know what she really thinks."

Lawless's relationship with producer Rob Tapert continued, likewise, on an even keel. Owing to the fact that he had to spend a lot of time in Los Angeles, Lawless and Tapert were lucky to see each other once a month and then only for a few days at a time. By design, their get-togethers were small, intimate ones, with dinner out with a small circle of friends the exception, and cozy nights together in private the norm.

But the producer does admit that his personal and professional involvement with Lawless has occasionally caused him to stumble a little in his judgment. "If anything, I'm trying to overcompensate and am finding myself being overly protective of *Hercules*. In deciding what stories go to which show, I had an incident where I took a *Xena* story and tried to make it into a *Hercules* story. It didn't work and I discovered, too late, that I had made a mistake."

Tapert, as it turns out, was not the only one who

felt that his involvement in *Xena* was taking away from the overall quality of *Hercules*. Sorbo, while basically happy with the way the good ship *Hercules* was being run, did voice some complaints that hinted at divided loyalties. "I seem to have an ongoing battle with the producers," he acknowledged during the early days of *Xena*. "They've taken my truly successful guest stars and put them over on *Xena*, which is fine but at the same time it's frustrating because they never bring them back to our show. I also get crazy sometimes with the inconsistency. Why can Xena, physically, do as much and sometimes more than Hercules can do and she's mortal?"

Tapert, in a recent display of candor, did not attempt to hide his personal relationship with Lawless. He would not go into particulars. But he did indicate that, from those early days forward, it was working out.

"Having a personal and professional relationship with the star of your show is a tough line to walk," he said. "It has not been difficult to balance out our personal and professional lives to this point. But ask me again in five years and I might have a better answer. At least, to this point, the relationship seems to be working out pretty well. And I think the big key to that is that we make a big point of leaving the work behind us when we come home."

And home is where Lawless would have preferred to be on one particular day during those early first-season episodes. New Zealand, normally a subtropical climate, had just turned wintry. Unfortunately Xena's wardrobe does not have the luxury of changing with the seasons and so, while the director plotted out the camera angle for a fight sequence in the middle of a flowering green hillside, Lawless was standing off to the side, wrapped in a heavy coat, wisps of foggy breath escaping into the blustery air.

At the director's word, she stripped off the coat and stepped into the scene. Moments into the sword swinging, the director yelled "cut," modified the camera's sight line, and called for a second take. And a third and finally a fourth. The scene finally completed, Lawless raced back to the sidelines and the sanctuary of the warm coat. She shuddered and said half jokingly to those around her, "It's no fun walking around in a frostbitten mini outfit."

"Sometimes I would go to my camper and it would be cold and I would see that bloody outfit waiting for me and I would say, 'Oh, no! Not today!' There would be days when there would be rain and hail coming down and I would be on the side of a cliff about to jump on my horse. Everything had to look good because that's the way Xena did things and there I would be, wet and miserable and freezing to death."

As Lawless would find out, wet, miserable, and freezing have their benefits when compared to some of the other unpleasantries she had to endure. On one particularly nasty day, shooting the episode entitled "Death in Chains," Lawless was standing at the entrance of a makeshift underground tunnel. She looked down the length of the tunnel and, in particular, at the watery, foul-smelling sludge on the floor. Lawless, ever the comic, rolled her eyes, held her nose, and sent a look to the assembled crew members that said, "You've got to be kidding!"

At the director's signal, Lawless began to slog through the tunnel. The reason for the foul smell soon became obvious as the actress began to slip and slide on the rat droppings in the watery mess. Things could not get more disgusting. But, as Lawless recalls, they did.

"All of a sudden a bunch of rats were dumped on me," she recalls with disgust. "It was awful! They were biting and scratching and getting caught in my hair."

Editor Field, who by this time had already collected quite a few hilarious outtakes, chuckles as he relates the part of that sequence viewers did not see. "This whole box of rats was just dumped on her back. She was laughing and screaming and just going nuts. I remember her last comment, just before they turned off the camera, was 'They're bloody nesting in me! That's disgusting!' "

When the scene was finally wrapped, Lawless made for the *Xena* medical wagon where, after washing off all the gunk and ooze, it was discovered that the rats had scratched and clawed a road map across various parts of her body. Although assured by the rat wrangler that the rats had no contagious diseases, Lawless painfully remembers "running right out and getting a tetanus shot."

As *Xena* progressed into its sixth month of shooting, Lawless had settled into a routine. And not all of it was good. Although flushed with the early accolades for her athletic prowess by trainer Wong and

the on-set stunt people, Lawless nevertheless continued to be the perfectionist and continued to find herself sorely lacking.

"I still did not think of myself as much of an athlete," confesses the actress. "I didn't feel that I
looked the part of a warrior princess. I felt I should
be bulkier and more muscular. And so I felt I had to
compensate for not being particularly athletic by
training long and hard."

Consequently it was not an uncommon sight during
those first few months for Lawless to finish a grueling
sixteen-hour day on the set of *Xena*, quickly change
from her leather fighting outfit into sweatpants or a
T-shirt and shorts, and run off to a nearby gym to
continue a seemingly excessive regimen of aerobics
and martial arts moves designed to keep her already
perfect body in fighting trim.

Lawless, unaccustomed to the realities of television
fighting, was finding cuts and bruises her regular
companions. Reports from the set, as well as outtakes
from the show, indicate Lawless was getting acciden-
tally coldcocked on a fairly regular basis. It was not
uncommon, off the set, for discolored welts and
bruises to be seen on her body. In order to speed up
the healing process, Lawless began to forgo some of
her allegiance to health foods and was regularly spotted gnawing on a piece of steak or other red meat.

"Things were out of balance," Lawless concedes
of her mania for physical fitness at that point. "When
I first started the show, I was doing a sixteen-hour
day and then going to the gym. I did that for about
eight months, five days a week. I knew I had to stop

it but, since I was so new to the rigors of television, I felt what I was doing was necessary.''

On the surface Lawless appeared little the worse for wear. She was on time, she knew her lines, and she continued to excel in her role on the show. But those who looked beneath the surface could see some emotional cracks in her chipper facade. She was tired. People could see that in her eyes. While still upbeat, some speculated that Lawless was not as relaxed as when the show first started. It seemed to many that Lucy Lawless was about to crash. And it was a speculation that was not lost on Lawless. ''I looked like a different person. In my own mind I looked like Xena should look. I'd become obsessed with my body and working out. But I knew that what I was doing wasn't healthy.''

Then one day her back went out. It happened right in the middle of one of her typical strenuous gym workouts. She doubled over, instinctively grabbing at her back muscles, and literally fell into a half sitting–half prone position, spasming in pain. Fortunately Lawless's back giving out would not turn out to be anything serious. Five days later, Lawless returned to the set to shoot the episode ''Altared States'' where, director Michael Levine recalls, Lawless was moving rather gingerly.

''Lucy had injured her back and had been out for five days. It was her first day back and you could see she was in a really good mood. She was happy to be there.''

So happy, in fact, that when a scene in that episode called for Xena to fight nude (in a makeshift flesh-colored bodysuit) after bursting out of an interrupted bath, she did so without a complaint. "We shot that scene at a waterfall," says the director, "and the water was freezing. When she wasn't shooting the scene she was sitting off to the side with her teeth chattering. But, when it was time to shoot the scene, she was perfect."

The episode also provided Lawless with some unexpected exercise. Normally, *Xena: Warrior Princess* episodes tend to run long and need judicious editing. "Altared States" came up a couple of minutes short. And so, under the director's guidance, Lawless did some prolonged runs across picturesque New Zealand scenery to help fill out the hour.

That Lawless was in such good spirits so soon after the back injury was an indication that the incident had served the purpose of driving home an important message to the actress.

"When my back gave out, I realized the way I was living was not really supporting the work I was doing," relates Lawless. "I knew I was killing myself. So I decided to stop running off to the gym and to limit myself to just exercising at home. I started doing a lot more walking and only worked out with small hand weights. I began to lose a lot of the muscle I had built up. But once I slowed down, I felt myself becoming a much happier and more relaxed person."

Lawless's discovery of a more balanced life and state of mind was fortuitous because *Xena*, like all new shows, was in a constant process of attempting to find itself. The producers and writers readily admit that the first couple of months were a fly-by-the-seat-of-their-pants shakedown cruise in which the show's tone was always being tinkered with.

"In the earlier scripts, we were really interested in exploring Xena's past and the ramifications of that in the present," recalls writer-producer R. J. Stewart. "But we saw early on that *Xena* was starting to take on a life of its own and that the character could not be tied down to just that one element. So a lot of those dark and brooding elements that were in the first five or six scripts were lightened, not because they didn't work but because we saw that we were getting more into Xena's present, her future, and her goals."

Producer Liz Friedman, a regular fixture in story meetings beginning with the first season, offers that she would often "find myself on Hero Patrol" when it came to defining Xena's constantly expanding character.

"My attitude is that I want Xena to be someone who is smarter than me, cooler than me and stronger than me," she recalls in explaining the effort that went into building a fully realized warrior princess. "I don't want to be watching myself on the television screen."

Lawless, halfway through season one's round of twenty-two episodes, continued to be like a kid in a candy shop—excited at receiving each new script, enthusiastic at the over-the-top physical challenges that were being thrown her way, and, on the days when daughter Daisy happened to be on the set, putting just that little bit extra into even the most mundane moments in an attempt to impress her daughter. The actress also stated during this blur of first-season activity that she was not daunted by the fact that she had not been able to totally find her character in this amazing Amazon woman.

"I'm still looking for her and it does not really matter what is on the page. After the first episode, I knew what the history was and that acts as fuel. But I also realized that Xena was in transition and on this journey and so I never quite know what she's about. At this point I'm basically going on feel and the rest of it is just happening organically."

And organic seemed to be the operative word behind the scenes, where Producer Tapert was watching Xena go from a largely angst-ridden notion to something multidimensional.

"We had a feeling, when we gave Xena Gabrielle as a sidekick, that there would be some opportunities for humor," explains the producer. "I don't think anybody ever conceived Xena as being totally dark and brooding. I believe season one has dealt a lot with Xena's guilt over her past but there have been moments where we've been able to slip bits of humor into the stories."

And that change was not lost on Lawless during a mid first-season moment of reflection. "Xena is considerably less dark than in her early appearances. But she will probably never be a barrel of laughs."

Laughs were definitely hard to find in the episode "The Greater Good," in which Xena's plans to defend a helpless village from attack are compromised when she is suddenly incapacitated by paralysis. Lawless set a high water mark for acting in this episode, with abrupt turns at irony, honor, and self-doubt.

Xena continued to be a progressive show during the first season by regularly allowing substantial parts for women. And while the guest stars didn't disrupt the show's tradition of showcasing beautiful women in revealing costumes, it balanced out the equation with strong characters. One of the strongest and most fully realized characters to emerge in the fledgling season was Callisto, in the episode of the same name, a psychotic blond who is out for revenge on Xena as payback for her family having been burned alive by Xena's army. It was a tough-minded episode, with Xena appearing to have met her match in another female warrior. How she reacts to, in a sense, looking in a mirror, made for emotional as well as physical high points.

"Callisto" will go down in *Xena* lore as the first time the warrior woman, in a campfire sequence, breaks down and shows any vulnerability.

"Lucy was very much into her character and very much into the emotion and the scene," discloses editor Field. "At one point in the scene Lucy erupted into this fit of nervous laughter. I was inclined to not use it but that episode's director, T. J. Scott, said that laughter was indicative of Lucy being really into the Xena character and with her being comfortable with the emotion of the moment. So we ended up leaving the laughter in."

How far *Xena* could go in the face of television's relative squeamishness regarding blood and violence had been an ongoing challenge for the writers. Throughout the first season, *Xena* remained a largely bloodless show, featuring comic book violence done up in quick edits and over-the-top sound effects. "It's really nothing to get too upset about," comments Lawless on that first season's action. "The violence of *Xena* has a humorous undertone to it. Everybody likes it when I cut a villain to pieces. Nobody is taking this seriously."

The first true test came with the season-ending episode, "Is There a Doctor in the House?" It was a very spiritual outing in which Xena shows her compassionate side while treating the casualties of a civil war. For Lawless, "Is There a Doctor in the House?" proved a physically and emotionally demanding exercise that forced her character to deal with the realities of war and death as she labored over battered and bloody bodies.

"It was a five-day shoot," she reflects with an obvious degree of discomfort, "and I can honestly say that it was one of the most intensive five days of my life. I was real busy in that episode. The atmosphere on the set that week was really intense and there was a lot of pressure. But I liked the fact that I was involved all the way through and not sitting on my backside with nothing to do."

The show features some graphic operating room sequences and brings out an unsettling but effective reaction. Not the kind of things that sponsors want to see wrapped around their soap suds commercials.

The memos from Universal started flying thick and fast after studio executives saw the finished "Is There a Doctor in the House?" Tapert and Raimi exhausted all their arguments in an attempt to convince the powers that be that this envelope pushing would not offend tender sensibilities. It finally reached a point where Universal said that either certain strategic cuts be made or the episode would not air. The *Xena* producers blinked.

''It was too bloody and too intense for some sponsor,'' says a disappointed Lawless. ''So we had to cut some things where you could see some of the operations happening. I was disappointed about that because I felt I had given everything I had to that episode. It was buried but we gave it a bloody good shot.''

And, as the first season wound down, *Xena: Warrior Princess* boasted the kind of numbers that made it television's Rookie of the Year. Since the show's September 1995 debut, *Xena* appeared in first-run syndication on 205 stations. In twenty-four of its first twenty-five weeks (including reruns) *Xena* succeeded in knocking off the mighty *Baywatch* in the overall ratings race and finally finished its season in third place, behind *Hercules: The Legendary Journeys* and *Star Trek: Deep Space Nine*.

Consequently Lawless went into hiatus receiving mountains of interview requests, critical raves for herself and the show, and the inevitable offers for offseason work. Most were questionable endorsements and movie and television appearances that Lawless quickly blew off. One substantial offer, to make a *Xena: Warrior Princess* movie, was also passed under Lawless's nose. But Lawless was not interested, preferring to take the definition of the word hiatus literally.

''I could have done a Xena movie,'' reveals Lawless, who preferred to spend her off time relaxing with her child. "But, to be perfectly honest, I don't think they could pay me enough to work through my hiatus. I would be depressed if I continued to work. A million dollars just isn't enough to pay for my sanity and my enjoyment of life. To star in something else right now would be madness."

EIGHT

Shell-shocked

L ucy Lawless had slept in. She got up around eight and looked in on Daisy, who was just beginning to stir, before going into the kitchen of her serviceable, but not flashy, four-bedroom Mount Albert home to begin preparing breakfast. Later in the day, her brother Dan would come over for a visit and Lawless, during a midmorning break, would engage in a minor workout of lunges and high kicks under the watchful eye of Daisy.

The actress's day might seem, to the world at large, downright boring. But, to Lawless, it was heaven on earth.

During *Xena*'s first season, owing to the long days and nights of shooting, Daisy would spend the lion's share of the week with her father and be with her mother on the weekend. During the hiatus, Daisy was spending a lot more time with Lawless.

"If I had spent my hiatus making a movie I'd be exhausted by the time it came to filming *Xena* again and that wouldn't be fair to the show," reflected Lawless on what she considered an all-important break. "But the big thing right now is that I get to make up for lost time with my daughter. With the long hours I had to work on *Xena*, I did not get to spend as much time with her as I would have liked to. So that was the big thing for me with this break; to spend time with Daisy and to just be a mom."

And a big part of just being a mom was to catch up on what was going on with her daughter's life. Daisy, then seven, was in grade school and by all accounts a bright, active, and attentive child. But what Lawless discovered, during leisurely walks around town and other outings, was the honesty in children and, in the case of Daisy, some post-divorce anxieties.

"At first she really hated that I was Xena," relates the actress, her eyes showing the pain for just a moment. "She just wanted all the celebrity and everything to just go away. In fact, she really hated the show because she blamed *Xena* for breaking up my marriage to her dad. She felt that people wanted me to be Xena and not the woman who was her mother. She was frightened because she felt a lot of people were wanting a piece of me and my time because I was Xena and that she had to share me with others. It was a rough time for both of us because, in some ways, she felt she had lost her mother."

In line with Daisy's fears, Lawless was having time

during the hiatus to come to terms with what celebrity, in a relatively short period of time, was doing to her life and to those around her. Initially she had taken to the publicity game like a duck to water, willingly doing endless rounds of interviews and, in typically straightforward fashion, deflecting the notion that Xena was quickly becoming a role model for women of all ages.

"Initially I felt awkward about the whole role model thing," she acknowledged recently. "I was feeling like some kind of anti-Barbie. It just felt like too much responsibility to bear. I felt it was all I could do to be a good role model for my kid and that I didn't need other people on my plate. Besides, despite what I was hearing, I've never really thought that anybody would seriously consider wanting to be Xena. To a certain degree that probably reflected negatively on me. Now I'm beginning to realize that the notion of being a role model is just something else I'm going to have to deal with. But I guess it was meant to happen sooner or later. It was just a lot sooner than I expected.

"But, in a sense, it's working to my advantage. Once I began to realize that I was a role model to a degree, I began to take a closer look at myself and my habits. As a result, I quit smoking because I didn't want women who looked up to Xena to think that smoking was okay."

The actress, with time to reflect, was also becoming comfortable with the idea of *Xena* being seen in a feminist light. "When I first began hearing things about the show making a statement about political feminism, I couldn't believe it. For me it had been nothing more than a bunch of people trying to put on a TV show that we liked each week. For a long time I was seriously afraid they would try and copy me and I was concerned about that. But, if *Xena* is inspiring some women to chase their dreams, I have no problem with that. I had one woman write me saying that she had gone out and bought a Harley-Davidson motorcycle, which she had always wanted but had been afraid to get, because of *Xena*. That just blew me away.''

As did the appeal of the show that seemed, after only one season, to have struck a chord across lines of gender, class and age. ''I just think there's something in the show for everyone,'' she speculates. ''We're trying real hard to try to appeal to the highest common denominator rather than the lowest. What everybody on the show is aiming for is for people to feel something. I hope it does become the next big TV phenomenon. I don't know what's to come but I do believe that, somehow, we've caught the next wave.''

Lawless, early on, also discovered her growing popularity, and that of the show, on the Internet and would occasionally log on to answer questions or just monitor the chat lines to get an idea of how well the show was going down. She was also good about receiving and responding to fan mail. But, by the end of the first season, time spent on that latter task had considerably diminished.

''A lot of the fan mail was wonderful,'' she acknowledges, ''but I was also getting a number of letters from people who had fatal diseases and that sort of thing and I was ending up feeling real bad for them and carrying this huge weight with me when I went back to work. I appreciate getting letters from people and hearing that they love the show but some of the things were just too sad.''

Lawless also had to bite her tongue as her celebrity status reached the point where she became fodder for the sensationalistic tabloid press. Lawless's life to this point had pretty much been an open book, and so the rags both in the United States and internationally went after the one thing that had the slightest hint of scandal—her romantic life with producer Rob Tapert.

The *Globe* in the United States, the *Sunday Mail* in the U.K., and the *Truth* in New Zealand all jumped on the notion, using conveniently anonymous sources and an alleged quote from Tapert's longtime companion Jane Goe to depict both Lawless as a heartless homewrecker who dumped her husband to be with her producer, and Tapert as a shark who shamelessly chased after her for years. Lawless never commented publicly about the tabloid stories but those close to her have said that she was both hurt and amused by the false charges.

Lawless was also feeling some annoyance at how her sense of privacy was breaking down. In her native New Zealand, she could walk the streets at will and people would leave her alone or acknowledge her in respectful tones. Fortunately she had taken the precaution of getting an unlisted telephone number. But, with the worldwide popularity of *Xena*, her parents have not been so lucky.

"My parents have started getting all kinds of strange telephone calls. They've had people ring them up at all hours of the day and night, saying that they were from New York and that they really needed to get ahold of me. My dad was getting really upset."

But, during her first hiatus, Lawless took a figurative deep breath in the face of this media onslaught and pressed on. "It hasn't been easy," she sighs, looking back on her big initial brush with celebrity, "but I'm determined not to get upset about it. The whole thing was really alarming to me at first. I've always fancied the idea of being able to go out in public and just go about my business. If things are going to change, then I guess I'll just have to get used to the changes."

While Lawless was enjoying her time off, Tapert, Raimi, and the *Xena* writing staff were hard at work prepping for the upcoming second season—a season that people would be watching closely. In its initial stories, Xena had already struck a fine balance; they were angst-ridden dramas with just enough comedic moments to keep the show from becoming incomprehensibly dark and brooding. That the mix of light and dark worked as well as it did seemed to suggest that *Xena* would continue to mine the same territory in season two. But while second-season story lines continued to play with the notion of redemption and the struggles to escape one's past, the writers saw in Lawless's, and in particular, O'Connor's, comic capabilities a chance to bring some whimsy to the series.

"We've been lucky with this show in that we've been able to strike a balance between the straight stuff and the humor," offers Tapert in response to the show's second season drift into comedy. "And it's not like we're forcing the issue. Although with *Xena* we tend to like things dark, I have no problem with putting comedy in if it fits. And with Lucy and Renee, we've stumbled upon two really brilliant comedians."

Lawless, after the months off, returned to the *Xena* set in a happy, revitalized state. Her constant but not vigorous workouts had maintained her well-muscled frame. Her time as mom to Daisy, while not curing all their conflicts, had at least put their relationship on the right road. And finally, great strides had been made toward coming to terms with her current stage of life.

"I've chosen to live in a rarefied atmosphere," she says upon reflection. "People react to me differently now that I'm on the telly. I'm becoming more of a misfit all the time but I suppose that's what I wanted to be."

Once back on the set, however, Lawless found herself in a familiar fantasy world of crew people, actors, and monsters that suited her day-to-day state of mind to a T. Given that, Lawless was in heaven when she received the script for the second season opener, "Warrior . . . Princess . . . Tramp," the first of what would be many comedic romps; in this particular episode Lawless ends up playing three different versions of Xena with, accordingly, three distinct personalities, even going so far, in a spur of the moment bit of improv, as to ride her horse sidesaddle.

"Xena had been very dour to that point," critiques

"Warrior . . . Princess . . . Tramp" director Levine. "This episode let her show her range."

Levine was on his third *Xena* episode and so had a pretty good handle on what Lawless was capable of projecting into her ever-expanding character. But even he knew that this assignment was going to be tough for Lawless.

"Lucy was actually having to play four roles in this episode. She was playing Lucy as Xena, Xena as Princess Diana, Princess Diana, and Diana as Xena. I talked with Lucy early in the rehearsal stage about how she was going to do each role. We agreed that there was a need to avoid caricature and yet give each character a distinct personality. Lucy started playing around with different voices and inflections. It took her a bit of time to find Diana but she finally did."

"I really like to be busy all the time," reflects Lawless on the challenges that episode presented, "and that was the one where I, easily, had the most to do. I liked having that extra add of pressure on me. It's under those conditions that I feel that I do my best work."

Lawless, as her confidence grew and her skills as an actress improved, began to loosen up a lot more than she had in the previous season. She was more prone to wisecracks and self-deprecating humor than she had been during season one. A good blooper reel had grown out of season one. A great blooper reel was already well underway only a few episodes into the new season. Robert Trebor, making another appearance on *Xena*, saw the highjinks firsthand.

"She was always goofing off in between takes and

having a lot of fun," recalls the actor. "One day Lucy and Renee just all of a sudden broke into song, singing 'Deep in the Heart of Texas.' It was hilarious to see these two women, dressed as warrior women, singing that song."

An otherwise subpar episode called "Giant Killer" featured a highly charged emotional moment when Xena and Gabrielle clasp hands. Field, always quick with an assessment, felt it was a defining moment "as Xena was able to let her guard down in front of Gabrielle."

As early season episodes flew by in a blur of titles such as "Girls Just Wanna Have Fun," "Remember Nothing," and the highly anticipated "Return of Callisto," Lawless seemed to have overcome any lingering self-doubts about her athletic ability and threw herself with a renewed relish into the sword fights, chakram throws, and the other requisite action and stunt scenes. And, despite the luxury of several stunt doubles, Lawless was taking her lumps and loving it.

"Yes, it's dangerous," says a proud Lawless of her rough-and-tumble work on *Xena*. "But, on a show like this, it's also par for the course. I've been lucky that I haven't been seriously injured but you do tend to get your share of bruises, whiplash, black eyes, and loose teeth. In fact, one day there was a miscalculation during a fight sequence and I got hit real hard and got a beautiful shiner. Well, they took me right off to look after it and the makeup people gathered around and were checking it out, so if I ever needed to have a shiner, they'd know the look of it when they put it on."

The meatier acting episodes were slow to click in but when they finally did, Lawless attacked them with a vengeance. "Remember Nothing" proved to be a taut "what if" scenario in which Xena discovers what her impact would have been on the world if she had never gone the warrior way. The success of "Callisto" and the surprisingly positive response to that episode's foe resulted in the second season outing, "Return of Callisto," in which Xena once again confronts the enemy spawned from the evils of her past life and discovers new levels of guilt, while exposing a heretofore unknown weakness in her worst enemy. "Return of Callisto" was a tough episode that brought out the rage and warrior instincts in Xena. In it, Callisto succeeds in killing Gabrielle's husband. Xena adopts a "waste the bitch" attitude, turns very hard-core, and ultimately dooms Callisto to an agonizing death in a patch of quicksand.

Bruce Campbell, who had already entered the mythological arena with a pair of guest-starring roles in *Hercules*, made his entry into the world of *Xena* for the first time with the episode "The Royal Couple of Thieves." The episode, according to Campbell, "was your basic Bob Hope road picture in which Xena is carrying the world on her shoulders and all I'm trying to do is get into her pants."

The actor, though he'd been hearing a wealth of Lawless stories from his friend Tapert for the better part of two years, had never met Lawless.

"I was actually talking to some crew members on the set one day and they indicated that, because I had done a period action television series (the late lamented *The Adventures of Brisco County, Jr.*) Lucy was interested in getting together and sharing some tidbits.''

Campbell and Lawless did get together during one of her workouts and went running together. It was then that the actor cemented his impression of Lawless. ''I saw that she had a real good sense of humor and that she was not letting all the celebrity surrounding the show get to her. She's a stunningly attractive woman who is, physically, as large as almost any other man. But she leaves that tough-woman-in-a-leather-outfit persona behind when she's not on the set. I found her to be this delightful kind of screwball. She laughs a lot and screws up a lot.''

Campbell also had the opportunity while in New Zealand to socialize with Tapert and Lawless and offers a skeletal dynamic of their relationship. ''They both seemed real happy. I know Rob is tickled pink and Lucy seemed to me to be happy no matter what was going on.

''I never really heard a lot about what Lucy's background was about when we were together,'' he continues. ''I never really got a lot of backstory from either one of them. When we would go out together, it was like they just wanted to get away from the business for an evening. They were more intent on getting a good meal and having a few laughs.''

Xena and *Hercules* continued to gather steam and Universal, finally waking up to the fact that they had a pair of highly exploitable franchises, got off the deck midway through 1996 when they struck a deal to do a direct-to-video animated feature, *Hercules &*

Xena: The Animated Movie: The Battle for Mount Olympus.

The movie, which would feature the voices of Kevin Sorbo, Lucy Lawless, and show regulars Renee O'Connor, Kevin Smith, and Alexandra Tydings, has a simple enough premise as befitting its children's target audience. Hercules' mother, Alcmene, is mysteriously carried away to Mount Olympus by Zeus. The plot thickens when Hercules' stepmother, Hera, and the superbeings called the Titans forge an unholy alliance to take over Mount Olympus. Hercules, Xena, and their respective comrades enter the fray, make a pact with Zeus, and ultimately wage a final battle against the Titans on Mount Olympus.

For Lawless, adding her voice to the cartoon feature was appealing on a number of fronts. The movie was something children Daisy's age could watch and enjoy. It would give her a chance to play Xena in a decidedly nonphysical way in the comfort of a voiceover booth. Finally, and perhaps most enticing of all, was that she would be singing three songs for the film.

To make a projected October 1997 release date, the voiceover work on *The Battle for Mount Olympus* would have to be accomplished right in the middle of the production schedules of both *Xena* and *Hercules*. That, determined Tapert, Raimi and everybody connected to both shows, would not be a problem. As long as everybody concerned was willing to give up their weekends.

They were and so, in mid-June 1996, Lawless, Sorbo, and company gathered in an Auckland recording studio where, on eight weekend days in June and July, they would lay down the voices for the film.

The sessions, though serious business, immediately took on the air of a party. Lawless had not seen Sorbo for quite a while and the result of their reunion was an enthusiastic embrace. They were all dressed informally, a welcome change from their everyday "work clothes," which made for a looser working environment. All of the actors were working in animation for the first time and so that first day was spent learning cues, running through the script one last time, and, finally, recording the first voice tracks.

It was a long process, made longer by many takes, occasional blown lines, and laughing fits that would often ruin perfectly good bits. But nobody complained. Lawless, in particular, was very enthusiastic about the process. She liked the idea of playing an animated Xena and that she could be, if anything, even more expressive and over the top than her live-action counterpart.

Lawless was excited and more than a little bit nervous the day she stepped before a microphone, headphones positioned firmly on her head to hear the music, to sing the lush pop ballad, "What Do I Do Now." All the years of fantasizing a singing career, her short-lived attempt at opera, and those childhood days of singing into imaginary microphones suddenly crystallized into one reality as Lawless opened her mouth and sang professionally for the very first time. The actress would later report that she quickly got caught up in the emotion of the moment and the lyrics of the song and, despite being nervous, was able, in her estimation, to do right by the song.

Tapert, who with Raimi coexecutive-produced the film, was a constant presence through the eight-day voicing of the film and expressed the opinion that "everything went real well" not too long after the sessions concluded.

It was around this time that Lawless's past came back to haunt her. The short film *Peach*, which to this point had been relegated to isolated New Zealand screenings and film festivals, surfaced in New York, to a couple of so-so reviews, in a lesbian-themed film festival, complete with Lawless's notorious on-screen kiss. Lawless, who had by this time already duplicated the deed in an episode of *Xena*, had no problem with *Peach* seeing the light of day. The folks at Universal, however, did have a problem with the appearance of *Peach*. And while they acknowledged the film and Lawless's appearance in it, a spokesman for Universal was quick to comment, "There will not be a *Peach II*. That I can promise you."

Xena: Warrior Princess cruised to the halfway point in the season a critically acclaimed series and a ratings blockbuster, with most of the adulation falling at the feet of Lawless. Interview requests were pouring in and Lawless again made herself available for every request of the publicity machine. The show had shown continued strength in the United States and, consequently, a number of influential national and regional television shows were clamoring for Lucy Lawless in the flesh. And so, as fall's unpredictable weather began to set in in Auckland and the production set shut down for its midseason break, it seemed the perfect time for Lawless to hop yet another plane for the States and conquer this latest frontier.

Lawless once again looked out the window as her plane taxied down the runway of the Auckland, New Zealand, airport. She was less apprehensive this time and more excited. The actress was on her way to the United States of America.

And a rendezvous with a skittish horse.

NINE

Break Time

Doug Wong cringed when he heard the news. He had received a telephone call from Lawless a few days before she was scheduled to touch down in Los Angeles. She had been excited and almost girlishly enthusiastic in chronicling what had been happening to her on the show and the current round of U.S. publicity.

"She told me she was going to do this skit on *The Tonight Show with Jay Leno*," recalls her martial arts guru, "and that she would stop by and visit at the studio right after she was finished doing the show."

When Lawless did not show, Wong assumed the show had run late or that she had been delayed by some press business. He was not too concerned. When he heard the news about the accident, however, that changed.

"I called her at the hospital as soon as I found out she had been hurt," states Wong. "She said she was okay. But she sounded like she was a little spooked."

And with good reason. The final verdict on Lawless's injuries was that she had suffered five separate pelvic fractures as well as assorted cuts and bruises. And while she was lying, largely immobilized, in a Southern California hospital, everybody connected with the incident was attempting to put their own spin on it.

A spokesman for *The Tonight Show with Jay Leno* came out on the side of the theory that the horse had thrown the actress. "You've got this animal that weighs twelve hundred pounds and has a brain the size of a golf ball," he said. "You just don't know what it was going to do." The consensus among the more than forty *Xena* fans in attendance at *The Tonight Show with Jay Leno* who witnessed the accident disagreed with that version. "The horse slipped," reported one. "It did not throw Lawless."

Lawless, continuing on the mend, had time to play the accident scenario over and over in her head countless times.

"I was trying to ride a Western horse English-style on shiny, painted concrete," she recalls, "and I had to keep bringing the horse to a trot around a corner. The set was tense because everyone was in such a rush. I could tell the horse was tense as well, but I didn't have the guts to stop it. I thought I would just be a trooper and get on with it. We did two takes that were okay and I agreed to do a third and final take. We rounded the corner and the horse slipped and we went down. It was as if someone had pulled a table-cloth out from under us. I was thrown clear. I was lucky not to be caught underneath.''

Leno, for his part, expressed his concern for and apologies to Lawless on the phone; he also thanked her publicly on his show "for being a good sport" and again apologized by saying, "I'm sorry for what happened."

R. J. Stewart was one of the first to visit Lawless after the accident. "I was devastated when I saw her," he sadly reflects. "She's such a lovely, wonderful human being. To see her lying in the hospital, in such pain, really knocked me for a loop."

Two days later, Lawless was pronounced by doctors to be in "stable condition" but they added that she would require a minimum four weeks' hospital stay and that it would be at least two months before she would be able to return to filming *Xena*. While concern for the actress's health and welfare was uppermost, it was inevitable that speculation would quickly run rampant on what impact her absence would have on the second season of *Xena*.

One speculation was that Kevin Sorbo, already stretched to the limit on *Hercules* would make cameo appearances in each of the remaining *Xena* episodes. More reasonable scenarios had Gabrielle taking over the lion's share of the action while flashbacks of Xena from previous episodes would keep Lawless in the picture. Yet another had the producers replacing Lawless with another strapping warrioresque actress for the run of her absence and then, conveniently, killing her off when Lawless was ready to return.

One thing was certain. The two-week hiatus in *Xena* production would end in a matter of days and something would have to be done. Producers Tapert and Stewart attempted to calm speculation by publicly stating that the already filmed episodes would take the series to the end of the year and that her absence would have a minimum impact on production for the remainder of the season. They did hint at the fact that some Gabrielle-heavy episodes would be conspicuous around the January-February 1997 air dates. That was publicly. Privately Tapert admitted, somewhat jokingly, that he was ready to jump off a cliff when Lawless fell off that horse.

"Our concern was really only for Lucy," recalls Tapert of the days following the accident. "But finally, when it was all said and done, we said, Good god! We've got all these scripts sitting here, and now none of them are going to work!"

Meanwhile Lawless was taking the first tentative steps toward recovery, which meant doing very little except watching a lot of U.S. television, being constantly on the phone long distance to assure Daisy that Mommy was alright, and, when her mind was not clouded by the aches and pains, trying to put the best possible spin on her misfortune.

"In a strange sort of way, it was the best thing that ever happened to *Xena*," she recalls of the post-accident publicity surge. "Falling off that horse really put me on the map. Before the accident, there were a lot of people who had never heard of me or the show. But the accident has changed all that."

But Lawless, while putting a smile on the pain, was

experiencing psychological fallout from the accident which was slowly beginning to play itself out in her more vulnerable moments during the early days of her hospital stay.

"No way would I want to go through that ordeal again," she would say to the small group of visitors who were constantly at her bedside. "It was much too painful and frightening to repeat. It's a bad dream and sometimes I don't even like to think about it."

The *Xena* writers, twenty-four hours after the accident, were facing their own bad dream: the prospect of junking half a dozen completed scripts. "Rob [Tapert] was keeping a real level head about himself during those first hours," remembers Stewart. "He was concerned about Lucy of course but he was also intent on saving our season. He immediately gathered all the writers together, sat us down, and set about trying to correct the problem."

Word of Lawless's accident almost immediately made its way to Auckland, where family and friends as well as cast and crew expressed their concern for her health before beginning to wonder how the remainder of the second season would be completed.

"I was a bit worried that we would lose our audience," recalls O'Connor. "Obviously people tune in to see the character of Xena. I was worried that, without the chemistry of two characters, we would lose a lot of our loyal followers."

Tapert, Stewart, and company were casting around for a game saver when they found part of the solution right under their nose. Prior to the hiatus, Lawless had just completed a tantalizing story line, including the

episode "Intimate Strangers," in which Callisto once
again appears and, as these things often happen, ends
up swapping bodies with Xena. The writers immediately decided to expand that plot into a two-story arc,
the second element of which (the episode "Ten Little
Warlords") would focus completely on Xena acting
out in Callisto's body and effectively mask the fact
that Lawless was not in the picture.

Hudson Leick, who plays Callisto, was immediately signed to finish the second part of the story and
flown to Auckland where, the actress reported after
the fact, she faced her biggest acting challenge.

"It's really hard to play someone else's character,"
explains Leick of her out-of-body experience. "I had
to imitate Lucy Lawless playing Xena and that's a
tough role to play. It's much easier to play a bad guy.
When you're a good guy you have to constantly be
aware that you can never look dumb. I gained new
respect for how tough a job Lucy has."

The writers continued trying to salvage *Xena*'s second season with an emphasis on trying to save already
completed scripts. One such script, entitled "Des-
tiny," had some possibilities. In it Xena dies, comes
back in the body of one of the many gods and deities
that occupy Xena's world, and is brought back at the
end of the hour as Xena.

"Someone suggested, 'What if we leave her dead
at the end of the hour, add a TO BE CONTINUED, and
have her come back in an episode called 'All of Me'
in which she comes back in the body of [semiregular]
Iolaus?' We banged out the 'All of Me' script and
managed to turn what most people would consider

serious business into a comedy,'' Stewart remembers.

Once the timetable for Lawless's return was established, additional scripts were crafted in which Gabrielle and other characters would take the lead in the action elements, leaving Xena to play a less physical role.

Tapert was pleasantly surprised with the results of the writers' attempts at a quick fix. ''What it turned into was an interesting opportunity to make some changes in interesting material, have people do some different things—spin a different arc and actually do some interesting things. The writers made lemonade out of lemons and Lucy's injury forced us to do things that we wouldn't have done otherwise.''

Stewart, likewise, was happy with the way things turned out. ''We really dodged a lot of bullets. We very easily could have found ourselves dead in the water.''

Lawless, a couple of weeks into her convalescence in California, was beginning to suffer the effects of being immobilized and bedridden. It was nothing a visitor could see, but Lawless, who was chafing at the confinement, knew her body was beginning to react to all the inactivity.

''I had been totally immobile for so long that my muscles were beginning to atrophy,'' she recalls. ''But there was never a doubt in my mind that I would recover and that I would be healthy again and there was never any doubt that I was going to walk again.''

In fact Lawless had made enough of a recovery that, a mere three weeks into her convalescence, she called up Jay Leno and requested a second chance at doing his show. Lawless, moving less like a fighting woman but still managing a bit of a swagger and a wiggle in her hips, walked onto the stage October thirtieth to thunderous applause and was greeted by Leno. Her segment was a joke-filled give-and-take centering around the accident. Leno once again apologized profusely and thanked her for giving him a second chance.

True to her word, Lawless walked carefully out of the hospital, producer Tapert at her side, early in November 1996, en route to the airport and an uncomfortable flight back to New Zealand. "I felt I could have walked without the use of crutches at that point but the doctors did not want me to go completely without them yet."

Having arrived home, Lawless settled into a routine of bed rest punctuated by gradual but progressively more taxing physical activity. It was not uncommon during this period to spy Lawless gingerly emerging from her car and, occasionally with crutches but more frequently without them, make the rounds of shopping.

Daily laps in a pool, with the aid of a special flotation device and special water-friendly dumbbells, were also part of the process of rebuilding muscles. So was kick boxing.

"Walking was tough," she says as she recalls those first post-hospital steps. "I could barely walk a kilometer. The bones were the least of my worries. I've got good hips and I drank a lot of milk as a kid so that prevented me from snapping anything. It's the soft tissue I'm concerned about and am working on building up again. This has actually turned into a golden opportunity to rebuild my body in a more functional manner.''

The recovery period also turned into a golden opportunity for Lawless to spend more time with Daisy and effectively deal with the problems she was having with her mother's fame. "She's a bit quiet about how she feels," says Lawless, referring to the fence-mending that occupied her time with her daughter. "She was bothered by the fact that the kids at school were always asking her if her mother is Xena. A part of her is quite proud of what I do but, to a point, she does not want any part of it. I feel like I was able to sort out a lot of things with my daughter and I feel I'm a much better mother now.''

During her recovery, Lawless would occasionally stop by the *Xena* set to observe how the show was carrying on without her. She was mobbed, carefully of course, and the look on her face reflected how excited she was to be back in the environment as did the fact that she could barely contain herself from picking up her sword and slaying some ancient foes. Lawless had already been filled in on how the writers were covering for her absence. When she saw the episodes actually being filmed quite smartly without her, she was doubly impressed. "What can I say," she said, laughing at the unique situation, "they've done a great job of covering my ass while my ass was broken.''

By year's end, Lawless had recovered sufficiently to agree to go back to the United States to finish up some press obligations. And, at the same time, to act on a girlhood fantasy to appear in a television sitcom. Fortuitously, in the show *Something So Right* Lawless appeared to have found the perfect platform. As a running gag on *Something So Right* the character Stephanie (played by Christine Dunford) is an actress on a TV series called *Thena: Warrior Goddess*. Playing herself, in a hilarious cameo, Lawless tracks down Stephanie and threatens to pummel her in Xenalike fashion for ripping off *Xena*. The appearance was vintage Lawless, a slightly self-effacing, yet bigger-than-life bit that harkened back to her Funny Business days and was easily the shining light in that week's episode. The immediate feedback from viewers, and not just die-hard *Xena* fans, was good and indicated that, in the long term, Lawless would have an audience beyond *Xena*.

Lawless also used this time in the States to schmooze local programmers at a national gathering of the Association of Television Program Executives. Her fun-loving nature had the normally uptight, business-oriented executives rolling with laughter and gushing with enthusiasm about how well *Xena* was doing in their markets. "I can't believe all the fuss they were making over me," she recalls of that event. It was also during that visit that Lawless expressed some lingering doubts about everything that had happened to her. "I guess I'm just being paranoid but I have this fear that it's all about to end. It's all been just too perfect so far."

During this stateside visit, Lawless made a quick stopover in New York. She stayed at the swank Four

Seasons Hotel and for the first time registered under the assumed name of Irma McHugh. From the posh suite, Lawless conducted yet another round of interviews and solidified the long-simmering Internet rumor that she would be starring in a New York production of the '50s musical *Grease* in the role of Rizzo.

Lawless explains that the chance at the *Grease* role came about rather innocently on a previous press junket when the actress appeared on Rosie O'Donnell's talk show. O'Donnell, who had played Rizzo in *Grease* years earlier, had heard about Lawless's singing ability and persuaded her to do an impromptu tune.

"It was all a complete surprise," Lawless confesses. "During our chat she told me she had been in *Grease*. I asked her what role she had played and she said, 'Rizzo of course!' " At that point it had been good fun and nothing more. But after the show and in the weeks that followed, she thought more and more about the possibility of expanding into areas like musical theater. Little did Lucy know, the producers of the latest incarnation of *Grease* had a similar idea.

"As it turned out, the *Grease* producers happened to be tuned in to the Rosie show the day I was on and had heard me sing. They liked the idea of my taking on the role of Rizzo. I thought about it. I knew they were interested in me because they always tend to wheel in the latest hot celebrity for something like this. But I thought, Why the heck not? This will be a new kind of experience for me and there really isn't enough time to do anything else with my time off and still have a chance to be with my daughter and relax.''

Calls were made. The show's producers, Fran and Barry Weissler, met with Lawless's managers. Terms were discussed and the result was Lucy Lawless in a seven-week run of *Grease* in September and October 1997 at New York's famed Eugene O'Neill Theater.

''This is my childhood dream,'' said an overjoyed Lawless once the contracts were signed. ''I didn't know how it would come about because of time constraints and a commitment to the series and all. But it has.''

Lawless met with the producers and director to line up a rehearsal and performance schedule that would not disrupt the production of *Xena*. It was agreed that, once Actor's Equity made the expected allowances for her to star in a stateside production, Lawless would come to New York in early August for rehearsals.

''Fortunately I'm a quick study,'' she revealed after the meeting. ''Because I'm only going to have two weeks of rehearsals before we go to New York and do the play for seven weeks.''

Lawless seemed confident, at the time, of her ability to learn lines, music, and cues in such a short period of time. But she was not completely fearless at the prospect of conquering another world. ''I'm not afraid of critics. I can only either be completely fantastic or I will fail miserably. I haven't completely failed yet. But I do live in fear.''

Grease, for now, was still many months away but Lawless knew which side her bread was buttered on and was never too far away from *Xena*'s sphere of influence. Hence her standing backstage, early in January, at the Burbank Hilton Hotel Convention Center, where the first Hercules and Xena Convention, entering its second day, was primed to celebrate her appearance. Lawless, dressed in a skintight, electric sky blue outfit, was excited. If there were any nerves surrounding the actress, you could not tell. She was having a bit of a giggle with boyfriend Tapert who, in an appearance earlier in the day, had been blindsided by an overzealous fan during a question and answer period with the inquiry, "When are you going to marry Lucy?" Tapert, the master of cool under pressure, responded, "When we do, you'll be the first one to know." Lucy was playfully speculating how far into her Q&A she would be when asked a similar question. Good-natured bets were made shortly before a scattering of clips from *Xena* episodes signaled her entrance.

The packed hall, to the tune of an estimated two thousand fans, erupted into applause. People rushed the stage and flashbulbs popped. Lawless beamed as the applause went on for several minutes. She quickly settled into the Q&A routine, scoring points as a charming and witty personality who appeared quite at home with the adulation. The questions ran a fairly predictable course—favorite episode, how the stunts are done, the lesbian stuff, working with Renee and Hudson, and finally, from somewhere in the back of the hall . . .

"When are you and Rob going to get married?"

"I don't want to talk about that," chuckled Lawless, putting a lighthearted rather than annoyed spin on her response. "Next question."

Lawless continued fielding questions with the skills of a polished pro. After forty minutes, the convention organizers stepped up and tried to relieve her of her post. Lawless refused their offer and went on for another fifteen minutes before finally relinquishing the mike and walking off to thunderous applause.

But her day was not over. She moved to an autograph table where she signed autographs for what seemed like forever. But she did not let the process become mechanical and faceless. She looked people in the eye, exchanged small pleasantries, and, despite her growing fatigue, made the fans feel like they mattered.

The actress had, by this time, been able to strike a balance between Lucy Lawless and her superhero alter ego. But while in New York, an incident occurred that once again had her attempting to sort things out. While dining at a New York restaurant, Lawless became fascinated by an argument between a man and a woman happening on the sidewalk right in front of her. At one point the man hit the woman and then walked away.

"My immediate instinct was that my Xena character would have shown that brute a thing or two," she confessed later. "But, as Lucy, I didn't know what to do. I wanted to intervene but I realized that I was thinking like Xena and that Lucy can't really fight. Instead, I went over to the woman and told her she didn't have to stand for that kind of treatment."

Lawless returned to New Zealand in late January

and, for the first time in five months, put on the Xena costume. In a way it was a magic moment for Lawless—slipping out of one skin and into another. Physically she felt she was ready. "I've built up my tolerance to pain," she confidently explained at the time of her return to the show. "Now I can suffer all sorts of torture without complaining."

There was a round of applause when Lawless stepped onto the *Xena* set once again, for the episode "The Quest." She was thankful, embarrassed, and uttered an epithet that reduced the assembled crew and cast to hysterical laughter. The episode's director, Michael Levine, finally broke it up, calling out, "Okay people. Let's get to work."

It was business as usual. Well, almost.

"It was strange shooting a *Xena* episode without much Lucy in it," recalls Levine of that episode's filming, which included the story's Amazon funeral sequence being temporarily halted on account of rain. "But, at that point, she was not up to doing much. She was still very tender and you could tell that her stamina was not there. But she was in great spirits and very happy to be back on the set."

Lawless did not jump full bore back into the action. She did pick up the sword fairly quickly and, although her timing was understandably off, she was quick to move back into fighting mode. Her first toss with the chakram sailed wildly but managed to stay in camera frame. Lawless insisted on doing as many of her own stunts as she could, and, while her still-fragile pelvis forced her to tone down the kicks, the consensus was that Lawless, only a couple of days back into the routine, was working well within striking distance of her peak physical skills. But Lucy Lawless's comeback was not quite complete.

Physically, she was ready to ride the horse. But the first few attempts at her doing so ended with Lawless shaking her head, muttering, "I'm not ready," and backing away. It was not intregal to the story lines that rounded out the second season. But, while nobody said so publicly, a lot of people were wondering if and when Xena would ride again. Lawless felt she would but she also admitted to having a bit of a block about getting on a horse again.

"I refused to get on a horse," says Lawless, looking back on that stumbling block. "I was not going to be pushed into it. I felt I had to recover fully before I attempted that. There was really no reason why I could not ride again. It was just psychological. But I felt strongly that I could not let people down and so I knew that, eventually, I would get back on that horse."

TEN

New Horizons

"I don't think I'll ever get on a horse again without thinking about Christopher Reeve," lamented Lucy Lawless as she sat on the sidelines watching stunt doubles tackle her riding scenes not long after she returned to the *Xena* set. "I can't not do everything so I'm going to get back on that horse. It's important for me to give myself that challenge, otherwise I'm going to be frightened forever."

Fortunately Lawless's injury had forced the *Xena* writers to make changes that guaranteed that she would not be rushed back into the saddle. "By the time Lucy came back to the show," recalls producer Tapert, "we were already committed to numerous scripts with Xena on a boat. In the coming year Lucy will be on horses on a more regular basis."

But, while Lawless was in no hurry, she eventually

reached a point in her own mind where she had to give it a shot.

Lucy Lawless approached the horse with a nervous, tight smile on her face. Trainers and stunt coordinators, who had been cracking wise before Lawless appeared, had now gone largely silent, only occasionally making encouraging small talk with the actress and gentling the horse. It had been some weeks since Lawless had returned to the show. The sword fighting, the kicks, and the running and jumping had slowly come back round into shape. But the actress had remained timid at the prospect of getting back on a horse.

"I knew I would have to do it at some point," she remembers, "and I felt if I didn't I would be letting a lot of people down."

Xena's writers had done a workmanlike job of easing Lawless back into the physical aspects of the show, consulting with her before writing in a stunt or an action sequence. But the reality was that the writers were in a sense spoiled, and so were chomping at the bit to write Xena as the total fighting woman she had come to be known as. "The writers had always felt that, 'Well, if Lucy can do this, why can't she do this?' " recalls the actress. "Their imaginations were geared to running totally wild."

Lawless walked up to the horse and stroked its head and muzzle. The animal stirred slightly at her touch, flicking its tail, and shuffling its feet back and forth. Lawless climbed astride in one quick motion and took the reins in her hands. Lawless guided the horse into a walk, gradually worked it up to a fast walk, then a trot, and, within an hour, to nearly a full gallop. The last bit of fear turned to giddy nervousness and finally joy at the fact that she was up and riding again.

"It just felt good to be able to ride again," she reflects. "It was like it made my return complete."

Lawless's recovery infused the remainder of the second season with a renewed energy, with the writers even more intent on experimentation and pushing the envelope in terms of what Xena could and would do.

Easily one of the more imaginative outings of that rollercoaster second season was "The Xena Scrolls," in which a bit of time travel finds Xena and Gabrielle in another time and in the guises of an Indiana Jones–style explorer [O'Connor] and a damsel in distress [Lawless]. "The Xena Scrolls" proved to be a nonstop hoot to film. Squeals of delight could be heard coming from the wardrobe department as Lawless was being dressed more modern—and rather dowdy—in period clothing and glasses. In another part of the set, howls of laughter were greeting O'Connor's attempts at puffing on a cigar which resulted in much gagging and retching. "It was pretty hilarious," recalls O'Connor of this episode that gave her and Lawless the opportunity to stretch.

Another second season high point proved to be the wildly outrageous and more than a little controversial "A Day in the Life." As the title suggests, this episode follows Xena and Gabrielle through a typical twenty-four hours in their lives. And that typical day featured the now-legendary bathtub sequence in which the women bathe together and soap each other down. Lawless recalls the experience as being one long laugh fest, focusing on everything from the temperature of the water, to how much or little they were to wear in the scene, to how many people would be allowed on the set when the scene was filmed.

"I was a bit nervous going into that scene," recalled O'Connor after the fact. "But I felt very comfortable around Lucy so it wasn't a problem at all."

If there was a problem, it was with that sequence adding fuel, albeit good-natured, to the lesbian subtext that seems to run through *Xena*. In past outings, the pair have cheek kissed, pulled each other's boots off, and slept in the same bed. And then there was the famous Xena kissing another woman scene that set tongues a-wagging. The sexual ambiguity had become such a nonissue with the show's creators by this time that an audible groan arose when the same old questions resurfaced following the bathtub sequence.

"The gay thing is definitely there," says Tapert, patiently addressing the issue one more time. "Certainly there's the belief that Xena and Gabrielle are having sexual relations."

Lawless on the subject is slightly more defiant. "We're aware of the fact that the issue is out there and we're not afraid of it. This is a love story between two people. What they do on their own time is none of the other person's business and what they do together is nobody's business."

Xena, despite the unexpected injury to Lawless, continued to move along, ratingswise, at a monstrous clip, pushing such venerable shows as *Star Trek* and *Baywatch* well to the rear in the syndication race. But

Tapert was far from satisfied with how Universal was treating his warrior princess, especially in the all-important arena of merchandising and publicity.

"Universal is getting higher ratings with *Xena* than *Baywatch* ever got," grouses Tapert in a 1997 interview, "but the show isn't getting one-tenth the publicity. With *Xena* they have a real brand name and I don't think they've been able to exploit it the way they should have."

Tapert's trouncing of Universal may not be completely warranted. Well through the second season, the studio's executives had been regularly sending him queries about Lawless doing a Xena film during her hiatus, a notion no doubt fueled by the fact that Kevin Sorbo had already agreed to do his first film, *Kull the Conqueror*, during his upcoming hiatus from *Hercules*. But the idea of spending her much-valued free time doing a movie, possibly on the other side of the world, still did not sit well with Lawless, who did not wish to set back her relationship with her daughter Daisy, now feeling more comfortable with having a warrior princess for a mother.

"She's sort of bored with her mother's work at this point," chuckled Lawless. "She's real cool when the kids want to talk up her mother being Xena and all. It isn't a big deal when her mother goes to work as Xena each day. As far as she's concerned, I might as well be working in a bank. Things are fine between us now but I still don't get as much time with her as I would like, so I'm not about to be away from her doing a movie when I'm off from *Xena*."

Lawless and former husband Garth continued to

have an amicable post-divorce relationship. If there ever was any animosity, none surfaced, and when they did get together, usually when Lawless picked up Daisy for the weekend, they were as friendly as a divorced couple could possibly be. Lawless, when pressed about post-divorce stresses, was quick to point out that there were none. This was much in evidence during the second season, when rumors began flying that *Xena*, reportedly searching for a better economic situation, might be moving filming to another country.

"For my needs, the show should stay in New Zealand," she responded. "My daughter adores her father. I would hate to make her choose between the two of us. This is as together as a separated family can be and it works very well."

Xena production moved steadily through its second season, inevitably running into that dreaded patch of winter weather. Lawless recalls one particularly bad two-week period when the weather gods were especially angry. "It was cold and it was rainy. It seemed like I was always up to my shins in mud. There were days I would crawl out of the mud, hide under a coat, and would feel the hail beating down on me. There was one day where I stood in wet sand for eight hours straight and then had to climb up a tree and jump out of it."

But Lawless knew that every sign was pointing to the fact that she'd better get used to it. *Xena* was continuing to trounce the opposition. Tapert was reporting to anyone who would listen that "*Xena* could have a very long run, well into the year 2000 and, ideally, six full seasons.''

And the reason for what he predicted would be a long run rested on the strength of Xena and Gabrielle. ''The show is about the relationship between those two characters and that relationship is constantly changing.''

Lawless had to agree. In her later evaluations of *Xena*, based on two full seasons of escapades, she found her character ''to have the devil in her gut, the angel in her heart, and her head trying to get the two sides together.''

''*Xena* is constantly evolving,'' she stated. ''There's always new influences coming into the writers' lives and mine. We're constantly daring and we're always trying to twist some line or plot. We don't aim to be politically correct and we're not content to let the audience get comfortable with this show. I like the way the audience seems to think they know Xena better than she knows herself. It's all actually pretty simple stuff. Xena is a good person who doesn't think she is.''

Almost from its inception, *Xena: Warrior Princess* had been a show that, largely because of the openness of its star, was willing to push the envelope. But the question of how daring *Xena* could be and still fit in with the rather puritan attitudes of TV executives was always uppermost in the minds of Tapert, Raimi, and the *Xena* writing team. Story conferences would often erupt into outrageous bouts of story ideas that had a snowball's chance in hell of ever getting made. Out of one such conference, however, came an idea that, once the laughing stopped, became one of the most daring *Xena* episodes ever—"Here She Comes, Miss Amphipolis."

In the story, Xena goes undercover at a beauty pageant in an attempt to avert a war. During the overtly comedic proceedings, Xena catches the eye of a shapely redheaded contestant and, at one point, engages in an amorous kiss with her. It is only after the smooch that Xena discovers that the woman with the hots for her is really a man. In an attempt to add authenticity the producers decided to go after a real cross-dresser for the role.

"We wanted somebody who would look real as a woman," recalls the episode's director, Marina Sargenti, "and we also wanted someone who no one would guess was really a man."

The *Xena* producers and casting people looked at literally hundreds of drag performers, including such dual-personality names as supermodel Ru Paul. They finally settled on twenty-nine-year-old gay drag performer Geoff Gann, aka Karen Dior, whose credits included a number of porno films. "None of the other stuff in Geoff's background was of concern to us," says director Sargenti. "We were casting a role and Geoff was the best actor for that role. And although Geoff is known to a certain segment of the population, he's not widely known as a man so he was perfect for the part."

When she was told of the casting choice, Lawless was ecstatic. "Karen is an amazing performer as a woman and as a man. So I was delighted she would be doing the scene with me."

Geoff/Karen says of that first meeting with Lawless, "She had no hesitation as to the kiss. It was actually her idea to make more of the kiss than it was in the script. It was initially supposed to be a quick, simple peck. Lucy's idea was to turn it into this big, passionate kiss."

Dior and Lawless met for the first time on the initial day of filming for "Here She Comes, Miss Amphipolis" and immediately hit it off. They settled into a conversation in Lawless's trailer, a conversation that eventually turned to the life-changing moments in their respective lives.

When the day of the kiss arrived the set was a nonstop laugh riot as the fully made up Dior and Lawless mugged and postured in suggestive poses before going ahead and doing the scene. Sargenti, after the scene was completed, addressed the fact that the scene would only add fuel to the fiery speculation on Xena's sexual ambiguity. "The concern about Xena's sexuality is ridiculous," she said. "This is all good-natured, campy fun and nothing more."

During this period Lawless, for her part, was gradually coming to grips with the fact that success as Xena was slowly but surely putting up the wall of isolation that inevitably comes with celebrity. When the show first started, Lawless would actively check and respond to fan mail. Then the fan mail started getting strange and obsessive, so now her fan mail was being handled primarily through a service in Los Angeles. Her forays out in public, even in Auckland where people tended to leave her alone, had become fewer and fewer. These days she was traveling with the beginnings of the dreaded entourage and, more often than not, checking into hotels under an assumed name.

"The trappings of fame have taken me completely by surprise," she has lamented. "I'm not out in the real world much these days. I don't even go to the supermarket. I've got somebody to do my real-world stuff for me. I'm ashamed to say that I don't even know the price of milk anymore."

And for Lawless, always a gregarious person, the idea of celebrity forcing her into isolation was something she was constantly fighting against. "People are starting to notice me wherever I go and I'm trying not to get defensive about it. But I am beginning to find it alarming when I'm confronted with it. But I'm determined not to get cross or become reclusive. I understand that's the natural reaction to this kind of celebrity and I'm trying real hard not to go there."

When Lawless was venturing forth, it was usually to coffee shops, restaurants, and pubs where actors and entertainment people tended to congregate. To a large extent, these venues were still an oasis where her celebrity was largely ignored and she could be herself. As exemplified by the day she ran into Willy de Wit in her travels.

"I hadn't seen Lucy since 1993," remembers de Wit. "I was wondering what she was like and if she had changed. But she said, 'Hi, Willit'—that's what she called me—and we yakked around. I said, 'Well, you're really doing well.' She kind of shrugged and said, 'Yeah, it's great' and then she asked about the other guys [in Funny Business]. I thought that was a really cool thing. It would have been easy for Lucy to remove herself from her past and to just get on with her future. But Lucy's just not that way.''

Through her relationship with Tapert, Lawless was beginning to expand her horizons. She became a real fan, through her many trips to the States, of American culture—particularly hockey and especially the Detroit Red Wings (''my boyfriend's hometown team''). When she was not secretly monitoring a *Xena* chat line—and in one case getting kicked off for being obnoxious—she had her computer glued to ESPNet (an on-line outgrowth of ESPN sports television) for the latest scores and news of the Motor City's hockey team.

In fact, her mania for hockey became a regular part of her press persona. Lawless would regularly praise the team and speculate on its chances for the Stanley Cup as the season progressed and began to regularly admit that her wish was to sing the national anthem at a Detroit Red Wings game. ''The only thing I really want to do is the national anthem at a Red Wings game. I've always had this thing about anthems. I think it has something to do with my growing up Catholic. I've always loved the idea of patriotism and big old songs. To sing the national anthem would give me immense pleasure. That would be a real highlight of my life as I'm good at it and don't crap out.''

Also through Tapert, Lawless had made the acquaintance of Amy Andrews, the wife of a local Detroit radio sports director, Mark Andrews. Andrews, it turned out, had some pull with the Red Wings and offered to inquire about making Lawless's dream come true. Andrews discovered that *Xena* was a favorite viewing habit among members of the team and that they would be delighted to have Lawless sing the national anthem. The Red Wings were, early in '97, well on their way to the Stanley Cup play-offs and looked to be making an early play-off appearance in Southern California. A May seventh game at Anaheim Pond against the Anaheim Mighty Ducks, which would coincide with a Lawless promotion trip to Los Angeles, would be the perfect opportunity for Lawless to live out her dream.

In the weeks prior to her public singing debut, Lawless found time to practice singing the anthem, drawing praise from those who heard her impromptu rehearsals. Lawless knew that this was going to be fun.

"Ladies and gentlemen!" shouted Mighty Ducks broadcaster Toby Cunningham on May 7, 1997 as light beams crisscrossed across the darkened Anaheim Pond hockey arena. "Please welcome *Xena: Warrior Princess* star Lucy Lawless, who will sing the national anthem!"

As the crowd went wild, Lawless, dressed up in an outlandish Uncle Sam outfit complete with a tight red form-fitting bodice, a sparkling blue jacket, and an Uncle Sam hat, walked, a bit unsteadily, across the arena ice. Arriving at the microphone, she paused a moment, smiling in acknowledgment to the roaring crowd. The music began to well up in the background. Lawless took a deep breath and began to sing.

Her voice echoed through the rafters of the arena in perfect pitch, moving easily through the up and down phrasing and complicated pitches that often make singing the national anthem a difficult chore. As the song progressed, Lawless became more confident and animated, making expansive hand gestures. As she reached the final stanza, she peeled off the constricting coat to reveal her red costume in all its glory. Lawless launched into the final line, ". . . And the home of the brave." And lifted her arms skyward . . .

"I lifted my arms at the end because I've got these great long legs and I thought, with my arms outstretched, it would be a good look to finish up on."

One side of her form-fitting bodice slipped down and her breast was suddenly exposed to a good part of the arena, the assembled news media, whose flashing cameras caught the exposure, and the television cameras sending the game out nationwide.

"I had immediate coronary failure," recalls broadcaster Cunningham of the incident. "I saw my entire career flash before my eyes. I immediately cut to another angle but I guess it was too late."

Lawless was unaware of what had happened, as she was intent on completing the song, so there ultimately was several seconds of her unrestrained breast caught for posterity. It was only after the last words were out and she was on her way to the dressing room with a friend that she realized what had happened and pulled the top of her outfit up.

"Some people had been giving me weird looks," recalls Lawless, "but I didn't notice that anything was wrong until we got back to the dressing room. When we noticed, I wondered if I had exposed myself and my friend said, 'No. You're just being paranoid.' "

Lawless was embarrassed but felt, in the throes of excitement, that not much had been seen. The next morning Lawless awoke to a call from Tapert's sister, informing her of what she fondly recalls as "my out-of-bodice experience." It was on that same day, during an interview with radio talk show host Dick Purtan, that the magnitude of what had happened really sank in.

"You mean I've been flashing on national TV?" she said incredulously when informed by Purtan how much was actually showing. "I'm horrified! It didn't really come down. Only a little popped out? Oh, then, no big deal."

Lawless thought about it a moment and then decided that, maybe, it was. She expressed concern that her mother would be upset. "Oh, god! I don't need that kind of publicity! I'm getting plenty of attention as it is. That costume was just too damned small. To be perfectly honest, exposed breasts were probably the least of my worries. I was more worried about slipping on the ice in those stupid shoes!"

For the next few days the news media had a field day at Lawless's expense. Television and newspaper accounts were everywhere with photos of the incident much in evidence (although judiciously blacked out). Lawless supporters on the Internet entered the fray with Web site operators insisting that photos of Lawless exposed would not be available for downloading. But, sure enough, within a week some Web sites were proudly trumpeting the fact that these photos were available for viewing.

Lawless, however, remained calm and relatively good-natured in the face of this embarrassment, often cracking small jokes at her own expense, such as ''I've been getting a lot of offers to sing the national anthem all of a sudden'' and ''Obviously it was quite a bit more exposure than I wanted,'' secure in the knowledge that another scandal would soon heat up elsewhere and the tabloid and sensationalist coverage would go away.

''Hey, it happened,'' said Lawless as the breast incident began showing signs of dying down. ''Obviously I was mortified but now it's time to move on to something else. Something really important.''

Lawless had, by this time, wrapped up filming for the second season of *Xena* and was on hiatus. But, with the specter of *Grease* looming ahead, this time off was more of a working vacation. There was of course the quality time spent with Daisy and the special time spent with Tapert. But Lawless would need every spare moment to begin getting acquainted with the *Grease* script. The publicity surrounding her upcoming run with the show was already raging and concentrating, primarily, on the gimmicky angle of Xena slaying Broadway critics. Rumors ran rampant that the producers of *Grease* were attempting to fine-tune the musical and, in particular, the character of Rizzo, to add appeal to gay as well as straight potential ticket buyers. But the producers ultimately counted on the fact that the character of Rizzo has always played as somewhat ambiguous and so no refinement was necessary. While the press was having a field day, Lawless was taking this step forward in her career very seriously, which came as no surprise to those around her.

"She'll do fine," Tapert has predicted. "For her *Grease* will be something totally different. But she knows what it is and she knows exactly what she can bring to the role that other actresses can't."

"Obviously there's a whole other side of Lucy that nobody has ever seen before," says Bruce Campbell. "Let's face it, she's an actress, she's not Xena. She's already been challenged quite a bit on this show so there's no reason why doing *Grease* should be a stumbling block to her."

Tapert, in the meantime, stated that Lawless's upcoming *Grease* run "was not causing the writing team to work overtime" on the coming third season. But he did offer that some scripts were already done and that some strange dark turns were definitely in store. "Xena, this year, is going to be a little wrong at times," he warned. "And she's going to be wrong for the wrong reasons. Right now the studio is really nervous but what we have planned has the writing staff giggling.

"In the coming season bad Hercules and bad Xena will have a little fling. Callisto will come back a few more times but her mission will be completed and she will be very unhappy. The loving relationship between Xena and Gabrielle will be challenged and there will be a lot more new villainesses coming on board."

Writer Steven Sears, while not as specific, did see "a lot of bumps in the road."

Lawless, ever the optimist when it comes to *Xena*, could not hold in her enthusiasm for what was yet to come.

"Bring it on! The darker the better! I can't wait!"

ELEVEN

Star! Star!

How big a star had Lucy Lawless become by mid 1997? One need only look at the merchandising for the answer. While slow in coming, when the flood finally did arrive, of all manner of tie-in items, one could get very dizzy counting the things that were tempting the fans of Xena and Lucy. There were dolls (appropriately proportioned of course), "the making of" books, novels, comic books, fan magazines, Xena costumes, and mounds of coffee mugs, bumper stickers, and other assorted souvenir kitsch.

TV Guide, whose editors sensed something in Lawless and jumped on the *Xena* bandwagon early on, ran a one-off Xena comic strip in an August 1997 issue. Magazine editors, who stayed strictly with the camp appeal of Lawless and the show during the first couple of years, were beginning to play around with the concept of Xena as a kick-ass warrior. *Esquire*, in an issue that hit the stands in July, ran a short interpretive article on Xena as dominant woman and, to highlight the piece, a picture of Lawless in semidominatrix garb reclining menacingly on a bed. Even the normally staid *Newsweek* magazine got into the act when it proclaimed Lucy Lawless "a formidable natural resource."

And the notoriety has not been limited to the United States. While her homeland of New Zealand has been slow to come around, places as culturally diverse as London, Turkey, and Iran have been riding the wave of *Xena* mania.

But for Lawless, whose favorite pastime when not doing the show is playing at her kitchen table with Daisy, the media blitz is a mystery. "I'm a million miles away from all that. To be thought of as a cult figure makes me laugh. I'm just reading the paper and making tea."

Lawless, in any case, had little time to do more than be amused by *Xena* mania, as she was already well into the show's third season and going full bore. The actress, at this point, had already regained the confidence necessary to do all of her own riding stunts, which was just as well since *Xena* season three was shaping up to be as action-packed as it was dark toned.

The season opening episode, entitled "The Furies," was proof positive that Xena was going to be taking a few turns. In it Atrius is discovered murdered and, when Xena refuses to kill her father's murderer, Ares calls upon the demonic Furies to torment Xena.

This episode offered Lawless a wide emotional playground in which to expand her acting talents. She played the concept of going slowly but surely insane in a darkly sardonic manner that reflected Xena's plight as well as the emotional conceit that insanity lurks everywhere. But the real test of the actress's growing skills came when it was revealed that the killer of her father was, in fact, her mother, Cyrene. The look on Lawless's face said it all.

The season's second episode, "Been There, Done That," took the notion of being forced to repeat incidents in one's life over and over and thrust it into a tragicomic vein that, by *Xena* standards, had a fairly high ratio of kills. "Been There, Done That" makes some telling points in terms of what death really means to Xena and, with the apparent death of Gabrielle at its hub, makes for an action tale of some substance.

The often-joked-about all-musical *Xena* episode became a reality in the season's third episode, "The Bitter Suite," an operetta of music and over-exaggerated action and emotion. Yes, Xena did sing, quite a bit as a matter of fact, dispelling any notion that the actress, by accepting the demanding assignment of *Grease*, was getting in over her head.

As if things were not hectic enough for the warrior-actress, the creative minds over in the *Hercules* camp managed to suck Xena back into Hercules' world in an episode entitled "Stranger in a Strange World," the premise being that Iolaus goes into an alternate universe and meets up with evil Hercules and evil Xena.

It was during these early third season outings that, in an ironic bit of turnaround, a horse that Lawless had been riding suddenly keeled over and died. "It was sad and funny but I had just finished riding the horse in an episode and it just died. I guess I'm just cursed with an interesting and unusual life and the horse dying was just typical of that unusual life."

Lawless, around this time, was hoping that audiences would be getting the whole *Xena* picture in the third season. "*Xena* has even more of a sense of humor now than it ever did before and I hope that audiences are seeing that. There's more of a sense of satire and wild irony in the new episodes. I think people are fully seeing that Xena can be a lot of fun when she wants to be."

Xena writer Steven Sears echoes Lawless's remarks, stating that the show has finally overcome, to a large degree, that stigma it carried when it began nearly two years ago of being an easy critical target. "It should come as no surprise that *Xena* ran the risk, early on, of being dismissed as just another titillation show. But we've managed to undercut that notion with great stories, great production values, and wonderful acting. Sure, there are still detractors. There always will be. But we know we're doing good work."

It inevitably came to pass, as it had in previous seasons, that Lawless, a half dozen episodes into the third season, hit an emotional wall. Logistically *Xena* was no problem. She was living a mere twenty minutes from the studio by that time. She was spending an increasing amount of quality time with Daisy.

But, she reflected at the time, "We are always under the gun to get things done and we're always shooting wildly."

Lawless was familiar with the feelings and she knew they would eventually pass. She knew she could rely on her second wind but, in quiet, reflective moments, she began to feel an itch, born of creative tensions, that she felt *Xena* might not always be able to scratch. "The more people ask me about my feelings about typecasting, the more I say, 'Should I be afraid of this?' But I'm not. I get to do a lot on *Xena*.

"*Xena* isn't going anywhere soon," admits Lawless, "but Lucy Lawless does have other aspirations. I don't want to be fifty and walking around in my leather skirt, saying, 'Hey! Remember me?' I would like to go out on a high. So, we'll just go until it feels right. I would like to start other projects but I'll have to cross that bridge when I come to it. At this point I don't know how I'm going to feel after twenty-three more episodes. I could not be working any more than I am at the moment. So when would I have time to do another damned thing?"

But, with the rush of publicity surrounding Kevin Sorbo's starring role in the motion picture *Kull the Conqueror*, the scuttlebutt surrounding a Xena motion picture began to pick up a new head of steam. As writer Sears explains, the rumor of a Xena big-screen adventure moved up a notch on the scale of possibility during the hiatus between season two and season three.

"We've talked about it and it would be neat to have it happen. But, for the time being, we're so

wrapped up in doing the series that we would not
have a lot of time to do it even if everybody agreed.
Besides, Lucy works so much that it would be tough
to ask her to do more.''

By mid-July, Lawless had gotten enough *Xena* episodes in the can so that she could take a nine-and-a-
half-week hiatus and begin her *Grease* preparation
with two weeks of rehearsals starting in late July. As
a foreigner starring in a U.S. production, Lawless, in
compliance with Actor's Equity rules, signed a contract that would allow her to perform in the States for
up to six months. Everything seemed in order. Then,
a week before she was due to leave Auckland for New
York, she received a call from her management team.
Lawless stopped packing.

An ad had run in the *New York Times* on July
twenty-third stating that *Grease* producers Fran and
Barry Weissler had shut down the production of
Grease as the result of a dispute with Actor's Equity.
That organization, after less than detailed research,
had decided that Lawless had not achieved sufficient
star status to qualify her for the previously agreed-
upon contract.

But the producers were not about to give up Lawless without a fight. Within twenty-four hours they
had delivered a box full of magazine and newspaper
articles and magazine covers that indicated that Lawless was indeed a star and, as such, was qualified to
do *Grease*. Crisis averted, Lawless resumed her packing and was soon winging her way to the Big Apple.

Darlene Love, who plays the Teen Angel, had been
doing *Grease* for a while. So had Jeff Conaway, who

portrays DJ Vince Fontaine. Both knew about Lucy Lawless and her celebrity as Xena. They were realistic enough to realize that the lion's share of the attention on this run of the time-honored musical would be on Lawless, and they could handle that. But there was also the curiosity factor. Could this woman who swings a sword and dresses in revealing leather outfits make the transition from television to the Broadway stage?

If nothing else, the show's producers, and particularly Barry Weissler, seemed convinced that their gamble of casting the warrior princess was about to pay off. "Lucy brings with her a definite aura," enthused Weissler as the musical was rounding into shape. "Before she even walks on stage, everybody is wondering what she's going to act like."

Lawless, who continued to describe the character of Rizzo as "a less evolved form of Xena," claimed she was not looking to any previous performance in getting her acting together. "I haven't seen anyone else's performance other than Stockard Channing's in the movie so there's really nothing I can compare my take on Rizzo to. I don't feel like I'm trying to fill anybody else's boots. I'm just doing what I feel works for me."

For *Grease* director-choreographer Jeff Calhoun, the questions were much more complex. He had *Grease* working like a well-oiled machine. The rhythms and timing among the regulars were flawless. The transitions between dialogue, dance, and singing elements were set in stone. He was aware that Lawless was familiar with the material and had no doubts that she could portray Rizzo with the requisite amount of flash. The question that troubled him was one of chemistry. How would Lawless fit in with the veteran cast and would she create friction by being the center of attention during this high-profile Broadway run?

Those were the unspoken questions going through Calhoun's mind the first day Lawless stepped onto the Eugene O'Neill Theater stage for the beginning of rehearsals for *Grease*. Lawless was nervous but strove to be friendly and was soon engaged in joking small talk with the other cast members who, it appeared, were fans of *Xena* and wanted to know everything about the show. Lawless, likewise, was interested in knowing all the ins and outs of *Grease* and so the ice was broken.

In the ensuing days, Lawless was put through specific aspects of the production. While she would occasionally flub an exchange, it became quickly apparent that she had read the script and was well versed on her lines. The exaggerated dance movements, with their emphasis on timing and interaction with other actors, was a bit awkward at first but Lawless proved a quick study and was soon moving as part of a precision unit. Singing was the one element of *Grease* that Lawless was most looking forward to. And, on the days when she would run through her numbers, those privy to the rehearsals could see that there was that extra bit of emotion and determination running through the actress. And, as lighthearted as the character of Rizzo was, Lawless saw the character as someone just a shade too serious.

''Rizzo is a character that's born out of my own

personality," she declared not too long before the rehearsals started. "You can't help but make choices in lines of dialogue and song that reflect your own personality. I think I've adopted a sort of Sandra Dee persona for Rizzo."

Consequently it came as no surprise that Rizzo, in Lawless's hands, was shaping up to be an over-the-top, flamboyant caricature, which, while maintaining the time-honored qualities as presented by other actresses, was being presented here with a modern, nineties kind of twist.

While everybody connected with the production was singing her praises, Lucy was evenhanded in assessing her progress. "Dancing is the hardest part," she said. "I can dance as Lucy, but to fit into somebody else's choreography is tricky. I've also picked up some bad vocal habits along the way. That's why the producers and directors have been tutoring me."

By the end of two weeks of nonstop rehearsals, director Calhoun had seen more than enough of Lawless as Rizzo to know that she was ready for her first real test. Broadway-bound plays rarely actually open on Broadway. Instead, they open at out-of-the-way venues away from reviewers in an attempt to work out the bugs in a live setting before hitting the Great White Way. But, given the time constraints of the upcoming performances, Lawless would have to be content with a full dress rehearsal. And so, despite feeling comfortable with Rizzo at that point, the nerves sprang anew at the thought of performing even in front of an empty house.

Lawless stood backstage, fidgeting with her fifties

high school getup and nervously patting her art deco 'do. Her imagination was in overdrive. Out front she envisioned a packed house rustling with excitement. An audience made up, to a large extent, of people curious as to whether the warrior princess could handle a venerable musical. Lawless, in the midst of this major fantasy exercise, also imagined that a sizable number of the crowd were fans of her show and, consequently, they were in her corner no matter what the outcome would be. She was determined to treat this as an actual performance, and to not let even the most demanding of fictitious fans down.

The lights went down. The curtains opened on Rydell High School. The music began to well up. Lawless took a deep breath, said a silent prayer, and raced onstage. Where instinct and many hours of practice immediately kicked in. The warrior princess as high school smart mouth was off and running before an invisible forum. For Lawless, the next couple of hours were a blur. She remembered hitting her marks, executing fifties-style dance spins and twirls, and being smart and sassy in her exchanges. She also vaguely recalled being on key and in tune when she opened her mouth to sing.

Finally, Lawless basked in what she imagined to be a thunderous curtain call and clasped hands with Conaway, Love, and her fellow *Grease* costars before taking a final bow and waving to the crowd as she walked offstage as the curtain fell one last time. Backstage, she was hot, sweaty, and, above all, ecstatic. Her fellow cast members came forward and hugged her as they congratulated Lawless on her first run-through. Lawless, ever the perfectionist, calmed down and immediately began to nitpick her performance, figuring out things she did wrong or could have done better.

But in truth, Lawless's first complete showing in *Grease*, although not perfect, was also not bad. Director Calhoun pointed out some mistiming on some dialogue exchanges and some slight missteps when coming in on a song or dance. But he was also quick to assure Lawless that those were typical first run-through problems that were easily corrected. And, true to his prediction, as the rehearsals intensified, Lawless's performance became more polished and, in her own eyes, professional.

What those privy to the early rehearsals of *Grease* discovered was that Lawless, by her very presence, was having an effect, albeit subtle, on the overall production. While the energy level in the show had always been high, this edition of *Grease* appeared a bit more lighthearted in attitude and a shade more springy of step. It was as if the veteran members of the cast were finding something youthful and appealing in Lawless and were taking their cues from her. Lawless was now looking at "this Broadway thing as being a broadening experience."

The Broadway company of *Grease* continued to fine-tune well into late August, riding the wave of good vibes and a growing feeling that Lawless would be a legitimate addition to the show. Lawless, in moments of internal examination, felt the same way. She gave herself respectable marks for her singing and acting abilities and noted, all ego aside, that she did have more than enough of the required enthusiasm.

The rest of the *Grease* cast agreed with the notion that Lucy fit right in. Conaway and Love continued to be effusive in their good word on Lucy. "She's so much fun, she fits right in," reported Dierdre O'Neil, who played Marty. "She loves to mess around and take chances." Sean McDermot, who played the pivotal role of Danny and directly interacted with Rizzo, echoed those sentiments. "I get to dance and play opposite this beautiful woman every night and look into those big, beautiful eyes. I'm just a lucky guy."

Lawless, settled into a high-rise apartment for the duration, continued to spend time in rehearsals as the date (September second) for her Broadway opening approached. She was on the phone to Daisy almost daily, finalizing plans to have her come to New York for an extended stay once school let out. Her parents and a couple of aunts were also coming to New York, as well as a brother who was flying in from London. "Yeah," said Lawless, "I won't be lonely with all these people coming in and out of my apartment." There was also a little time for sightseeing and, when he could get away from *Xena* business for a couple of days, time for Rob.

New York was definitely going *Grease* and Lawless crazy. A series of newspaper ads began to run, some featuring Lawless in her Rizzo costume and one, a blatant attempt to hook the *Xena* audience, showing the actress in her *Xena* costume. Posters for the show were disappearing as fast as they were put up and, according to word on the street and the Internet, were being hawked at collectible prices. Tickets were going like hotcakes, many of them—fueled by Web sites trumpeting her *Grease* run—to *Xena* fans.

It was all part and parcel of a fantasy ride/love affair that Lawless was having with New York City. But never far from her mind was September second. Her Broadway debut. Lawless was still a bit apprehensive. How would the notoriously tough New York critics receive a television actress—especially one starring in a show as firmly in the campy, comic book vein as *Xena*—attempting to make the jump to Broadway? Would they praise her? Or would they bury her? Lawless had often speculated how "she might just go away after *Xena* and just have a lot of kids." Would a disastrous Broadway outing be the beginning of that reality?

With such thoughts running through her head, Lawless was excited, yet reserved as she awaited the curtain going up on September 2, 1997, at the Eugene O'Neill Theater. People had begun lining up hours before the scheduled performance. It was a festive line, with fans sporting likenesses of Lawless as both Xena and Rizzo. It was a scene that could very easily find a home in a *Xena: Warrior Princess* episode.

As was the controlled chaos of activity backstage. Actors, in various stages of dress and undress, were making final adjustments on their costumes, hair, and makeup. Director Calhoun was in constant conversation with actors and lighting people, offering last-minute instruction on cues, entrances, and where to move to ensure a specific number was in the spotlight. But it was all pretty much unnecessary at this point.

The rehearsals had succeeded in molding all elements of the production into one cohesive unit.

Including Lucy Lawless, whose backstage demeanor was a mixture of opening night jitters and excitement at this dream finally coming true. Knowing that Rob was somewhere in the house only partially calmed her nerves. Mentally she went over her songs, her dance steps, and her dialogue. She took a deep breath. She was ready.

The onstage call began to circulate through the backstage dressing rooms and hallways. Lawless primped one last time in her dressing room, making sure her costume was adjusted and secure (perhaps shades of the national anthem fiasco were still fresh in her head) and went out to mingle with the other actors. Conaway and Love had been through this moment hundreds of times before and so, with their relaxed joking, were a calming influence in those last few moments. . . .

Before the lights in the Eugene O'Neill Theater went down and the curtain came up.

The applause, already deafening, easily went up another handful of decibels when Lawless appeared on the stage. The first hour literally flew by. Lawless, as in previous performances, had latched on to the persona of Rizzo as the tough girl with a heart of gold and was running with it. She was totally in character as she ran the gamut from cynical to hopeful to vulnerable and back again. Her interactions with the other actors were crisp and believable. If there were any stumbles or miscues, they were impossible to pick up. And when Lawless opened her mouth to sing, her clear, emotional, and slightly over the top expressiveness turned her interpretation of the most familiar of lyrics into something new.

The applause was long, loud, and regular as *Grease* cruised through its larger-than-life fifties time warp to its familiar happy ending. Lawless seemed to gain confidence as the musical progressed and, by the performance's conclusion, appeared to be in a state of performing grace.

Lawless, glistening with sweat and a broad smile creasing her face, raced out to the front of the stage to take a deep bow and clasp hands with her fellow actors for her first Broadway curtain call. Once again the applause level, coupled with yells and whistles, rattled the rafters. The curtain came down as Lawless and the rest of the cast raced to the wings and embraced each other. For Lawless there were tears of joy and wide-eyed excitement as she gave and received congratulations for a job well done.

Lucy Lawless had taken the next step.

Later that night, the *Grease* cast and crew, in a time-honored theater tradition, gathered at Sardi's to eat, drink . . . and wait for the early editions of the New York papers, with their first reviews of *Grease* and Lawless's maiden theatrical effort. Lucy's opening night joy increased when she received an unexpected congratulatory phone call from Renee O'Connor.

"Opening night was great," Lucy breathlessly enthused the next day. "I have no memory of it whatsoever."

The excitement surrounding the opening night of

Grease immediately subsided into the typical theatrical schedule of long nights, sleeping in, and getting to the theater a couple of hours before showtime. Typical for everybody but Lawless.

The attention on *Grease* was still focused primarily on her, and so her days, early in the run, were still being occupied with interviews. There was also the random blocks of time set aside to be a tourist and take in the wonders of New York City.

Lawless stood at the gate as the international flight from New Zealand touched down at New York's bustling JFK airport. There was a bit of a cold snap in the air but Lawless could not have been feeling warmer, because the plane touching down had her daughter, Daisy, inside. The actress, now very much the anxious mother, strained her gaze in the direction of the plane as it came to a halt. Moments later tears of happiness came to her eyes as Daisy bounded off the plane, spotted her mother, and ran into her arms.

The following weeks were easily some of the happiest in Lawless's life. The bond between mother and daughter, and daughter with mother and father, could not have been stronger as Lawless and Daisy were inseparable. Days passed in a whirl of sightseeing as Lawless pointed out such sights as the Empire State Building, the Statue of Liberty, and the theater where she was working at night. Daisy, despite precocious attempts at being cool, fell under the spell of being in America and embraced the experience with all the childlike exuberance she could muster.

There was a real sense of excitement in the air the night Daisy saw Lawless perform in *Grease* for the first time. Lawless, knowing her daughter was in the audience, gave it just that extra little bit. And the look on Daisy's face was priceless.

Lawless, despite a dedication to rehearsals that were running morning through night, was getting a bit restless and so made it a point to get out on a particular night and, dressed preppie in jeans, a shirt and heels, made a beeline for the lesbian bar Meow Mix which, with its much-publicized Xena nights, had become a cornerstone of the show's unorthodox support. Lawless walked into the club relatively unnoticed and sat down at a table in a darkened corner. She admitted to those who accompanied her that night that "she felt like a bird being let out."

During the evening she talked freely about many subjects. When it came to the inevitable question of the popularity of *Xena*, she told visitors to her table, "I'm just kind of going with the flow. It's fascinating to see people get whipped up into a frenzy."

Meow Mix regulars eventually spotted their idol in their midst and began going up to Lawless for autographs, which she happily signed while shaking hands and answering questions about her take on the character of Rizzo. "Rizzo is a tough, hard woman with a heart," she told one fan. "It's a great role for me. They could hardly cast me as the good girl."

As the evening drew to a close and Lawless prepared to leave the club, she addressed one fan's question of how nervous she was about doing *Grease* and appearing on Broadway. "I feel it's time to risk it all," she said. "I want to be able to get to the end of my life and say I knocked the bastard off. There's no more time to be afraid.''

How brave Lawless was feeling at that point became evident when, after accepting television interview opportunities with such softball interviewers as good friend Rosie O'Donnell, Regis and Kathy Lee, and Larry King, she agreed to put herself to the ultimate test: guesting on the notorious Howard Stern radio show. Stern, a top-rated U.S. shock jock, had, in his own lewd and crude way, been an outspoken fan of Lucy and the show and so it seemed like a good opportunity.

Lucy, however, recalls that Daisy did not think so. ''I had bought the soundtrack album of Howard Stern's *Private Parts* movie,'' she chuckled, ''and showed it to Daisy. Daisy took one look at the cover of Stern almost completely naked and said, 'Mummy, don't go on that man's show.' ''

But Lucy did and was immediately put on the hot seat. Predictably, Stern launched a barrage of questions centering around sex. Although familiar with the shock jock's outrageous approach to humor, Lucy was initially taken aback by the slew of questions centering around lesbianism, anal sex, and whether she would consider sleeping with him. But she rebounded nicely and was able to counter his outrageousness with good-natured comebacks.

Surprisingly the Stern interview managed to reveal some insights into the actress that had, to that point, not been made public. She revealed that she and Garth ''were continuing to go to counseling together and attempting to make sure they maintained a healthy relationship because of Daisy.'' She also reported that Garth ''is very happily involved with another woman'' and that, in regards to her relationship with Tapert, ''I like older men and Rob and I don't use the 'M' [marriage] word.''

As a parting shot, Lucy laughingly remarked, ''At this point I don't have 'fuck-you' money, but I do have a 'fuck-you' attitude.'' The consensus, in assessing her appearance, was that Lucy had fought Stern to a hard-earned draw.

Through Rob, Lawless was being kept abreast of what was going on with scripts for the remaining episodes of *Xena*'s third season. And the consensus was that, once Rizzo made her final bow, Xena would be waiting in the wings and Lawless's work would definitely be cut out for her.

''There's some really grueling stuff coming up,'' she teased during her New York period. ''Emotionally it's really going to shake up Xena's world. We've got some risky ideas. But we're going to roll with it and, hopefully, the audience will hang in there.''

For the moment, though, Lawless was very much in her glory as *Grease*, largely due to her presence, continued to play to packed houses. The early notices had tended to be very good, and this trend continued. Lawless could live with the fact that all the reviews invariably mentioned *Xena* but took obvious pride in the fact that some reviewers were finally treating her as a real actress.

Lawless's happiness seemingly knew no bounds. But on October 2, Lawless and Rob Tapert broke a million hearts when they announced that they were, in fact, engaged to be married at a yet-undecided date.

Lawless's run in *Grease* came to its inevitable end. The last night was bittersweet. There was a real lump in her throat as she waited in the wings to go out that last time. Consequently there was more of an emotional edge to Rizzo that night than there had been on previous nights. The pathos in the role was more marked in that final performance. The humor and irony had been etched much deeper. And the audience that night knew the score and encouraged her at every turn.

Finally there was the last curtain call. The final tearful exchanges between Lawless and her cast mates. *Grease* was over. "I love Broadway," Lucy said, "but I like the constant challenge of *Xena* and I'm anxious to get back to New Zealand."

It was time to return to the real world of myths, monsters, and fighting women.

TWELVE

Return of the Fighting Woman

Auckland was in one of those in-between periods of spring when Lawless arrived home in late October 1997. There was just enough breeze to keep a moderate chill in the air. But the sun, in contrast, was riding high and shining bright.

It felt like *Xena* weather. And even with the accolades from her *Grease* run still ringing in her ears, Lawless had no sooner touched her feet down on New Zealand soil than she was already clicking back into a warrior princess state of mind. In the days after her return, although not totally withdrawn, Lawless had unexpected quiet moods in the midst of her more characteristic upbeat enthusiasm. Many perceived this as the inevitable emotional letdown after having spent seven weeks basking in the Broadway spotlight. Lawless saw it as just getting back into character.

Lawless spent the few days alloted her, before she had to once again report to the *Xena* set, getting her house in order. She spent a bit more time with Daisy as the youngster prepared to go back to school. There was some rare quality time with her parents. And, although by this time *Xena* mania had hit full force in her hometown, she ventured out on some shopping trips.

Lawless was truly reflective and, both inwardly and outwardly, upbeat about the future. For *Grease*, whether anybody wanted to admit it or not, had been a true test for Lucy Lawless. The pop culture landscape is littered with the bones of actors and actresses who, having lucked into one massive bit of success ultimately find themselves unable to escape that role and end up duplicating it all the way to obscurity. Xena could have very easily been that kind of role for Lucy Lawless. The show's success and a long run assured midway through a third season, Lawless had reached a point where, despite her desire for family time, she had had to use her hiatus to test the waters. If she had bombed in *Grease*, it would have only fueled any feelings casting agents and producers might have that Xena was all she could do. Which, to her career, would have meant a slow, painful death.

Lawless acknowledged the chance she had taken with *Grease* but revealed the risk was more personal than professional. ''I had always been terrified to sing in public,'' she said. ''I guess that's why I chose to do *Grease*. It really forced me to confront my fears.''

Critically Lawless had survived the Broadway test. At their least charitable, reviewers had indicated that Lawless had a natural feel for the more bombastic, over the top, lighthearted elements of the musical. At the other end, they were falling all over themselves predicting stardom.

Even before her stint in *Grease* ended, the expected rush of offers—and rumored offers—were run by her. The persistent notion of a Xena motion picture once again came up and, just as before, was filed away for future consideration. Some other fantasy-oriented scripts were reportedly making their way to Lawless for her perusal. There was even talk of extending her run on *Grease*. On a more substantial note, *Hercules & Xena: The Animated Movie: The Battle for Mount Olympus* would be released in January 1998, and early buzz indicated that the video would be flying out of video stores to rave reviews.

In the flood of offers that greeted Lucy upon her return to New Zealand was the not-surprising offer from *Playboy* for Lawless to pose nude. It was an offer that Lucy immediately turned down. "I said no. I won't do nude scenes in movies. Why would I pose nude for *Playboy*?"

But, for the time being, getting back to *Xena* was all that mattered. The first half of season three had been a monstrous success. The promised expansion of the *Xena* universe into even darker psychological territory for its lead character had to a large extent been fulfilled. Even that last bastion of critics, who held steadfastly to the notion that *Xena* was still ultimately a camp, comic book creation, caved in to the extent that they began to praise the story lines as daring and, by television's notoriously timid standards, innovative.

Lawless's first day back on the set of *Xena* was an all-out party. She had talked to some cast and crew people, either in person or by phone, since her return but this was the first time they had all been together. There were hugs, kisses, shouts, and more than a few happy tears. News of Lawless's success in New York had spread like wildfire through the New Zealand entertainment community and so the early hours of that slightly overcast morning were spent getting very little actual work done.

Lawless, ever the professional, had gone fairly quickly to her trailer and gotten into her Xena costume, joking that it still fit after eating upscale in New York for all those weeks. In between receiving congratulations, she had her head buried in her script, attempting to get her lines down for those first scenes of the day.

Finally, by midmorning, the party atmosphere began to die down and crew and cast members began to take their appointed positions behind and in front of the camera. Lawless gave some final tugs at her costume. She strapped on the scabbard that carried her mighty broadsword and strode onto the set.

It was time for the fighting woman to go back to work.

EPILOGUE

Lucy Lawless was light-years away from being a Warrior Princess on March 28, 1998, when she and Rob Tapert became husband and wife in a traditional Catholic ceremony held at the Saint Monica Church in Santa Monica, California. In place of her leather miniskirt was an elegant silk-and-satin ivory gown created by *Xena* costume designer, Ngila Dickson. And instead of her trademark warrior yell, there was a quiet "I do" when the priest asked if she took Tapert as her lawfully wedded husband.

Finally her warrior scowl, which turns gods and mortals alike to ice, was replaced by the very human image of Lucy dabbing at her eyes with a handkerchief during the ceremony as her daughter, acting as the maid of honor, smiled up at her.

The ceremony was attended by 340 family, friends and *Xena* cast members, who made the trip from New Zealand to be there on Lucy and Rob's special day. The couple glowed as the ceremony concluded. Lucy, shedding tears of happiness as she left the church, said, "This has been the greatest year of my life, and Rob is the finest man I have ever known." Tapert, likewise, was ecstatic. "I've waited 43 years for this day and 43 years for this woman." Renee O'Connor, also wiping tears of joy from her eyes, was effusive in declaring, "Lucy looked so radiant, she was beaming."

The wedding reception that followed was held at the ultra-ritzy Regent Beverly Wilshire Hotel in Beverly Hills, and featured a nautical motif. The multi-layered wedding cake was topped by an unusual bride and groom—the figures of a mermaid and the god Poseidon. The kitch-camp trappings included a gyrating Elvis impersonator. As a fifteen-piece band began warming up, Renee O'Connor, looking around the reception hall, jokingly remarked to her spruced up *Xena* mates: "After all the time we spend slogging in the mud, it's hard to believe that we all cleaned up so well."

As the reception began, Rob and Lucy, grinning from ear to ear, stepped to the dance floor and, as the band struck the familiar strains of the song "Beyond the Sea," executed the traditional first dance with their eyes locked romantically on each other. It was a look that said LOVE in capital letters. As the dance ended, Tapert, in an unexpected move, dipped Lucy and gave her a long, loving, electric kiss.

Everybody would later chuckle at the irony of the moment. If any man had dared get that familiar with Xena, he would have been beaten within an inch of his life by the Warrior Princess. But this was not Xena, this was Lucy.

And it was Lucy who responded by going limp—giving herself up to the romance of real life, which is every bit as marvelous as her fictional life.

Lucy . . . Log On

The state of pop culture in the nineties is often reflected on the Internet. Assuming that's true, then Lucy Lawless is pop culture in the nineties. Having spent far too much time perusing the best and worst that Lawless fans had to offer, I submit to you the fruits of my labor. These are the best of the bunch.

Ronny's Xena Homepage

http://www.cs.uni-magdeburg.de/rschulz/xena/articles/ html

Your basic one-stop shop of anything of consequence that has been printed on *Xena: Warrior Princess* and Lucy Lawless. Tons of domestic and international articles and transcripts. Updated regularly.

Tom's Xena Page
http:// www.xenafan.com

The total *Xena* playground. Tom's monument to Xena and Lucy contains a fat article and transcript list (updated regularly), fan fiction, pictures, sounds, trivia contests, and news of *Xena*-related merchandise.

Xena: Media Review
http://www.xenafan.com/xmr

A periodically produced roundup of articles and media coverage of *Xena* that does a professional job of excerpting newspaper and magazine coverage.

Whoosh!
http://www.thirdstory.com/whoosh/html

The name of this on-line magazine is the sound Xena's chakram makes when she slings it. The mag itself is an entertaining mix of essays, fan gushes, and insightful interviews with *Xena* behind-the-scenes people. A good, solid read that comes out pretty regularly.

A Whoosh! side site (http://www.thirdstory.com/whoosh'faq/) features answers to frequently asked questions about the stars, biographical information, episode guides, air dates, links to additional Web sites, and back issues of Whoosh! A good place to learn the basics.

Xena Online Resources
http://www.xenite.org/xenaonln

The ultimate playground. This is the jumping-off point for more than five hundred Web sites, mailing lists, and chat rooms.

Articles on Lucy
http://www.simplenet.com/articles/html

The title tells all in this regularly updated and quite thorough collection of newspaper and magazine articles, radio and television transcripts, and on-line interviews.

Gabbygab & Mariner's Look at Xena: Warrior Princess
http://www.simplenet.com.xen/index. html

A fun site that contains article transcripts, sound bites, pictures, episode lists, fan fiction, and links to other links.

Lily Valey's Home Page
http://www.radix.net/lily valey/index.html

A solid, if not overly spectacular, look at the *Xena* universe that offers fan poetry, news and convention info, chat forums, and links to other sites.

VIP Xena Links
http://www.pitzer.edu/departments/Career Services/ xenalink.html

VIP offers individual sites focusing on *Xena* characters and the actors who play them. There's also info
on the show proper as well as merchandise information.

A Day in the Life (of a Xena Addict)
http://www.xena simplenet.com

Great title. Pretty decent site. Xena Addict has on its
agenda articles on the show, *Xena* news, chat rooms,
and general information about the show and, in particular, Lawless.

Leesa's Smithsonian Page
http://www.ro.com/leesa/index.html

More of a fan club outlet than a place for insightful
information, this page does offer the occasional foreign article as well as a wide array of Xenaverse fan
club pages and net forums.

The International Xena Fan Association
http://www.personal.riversusers.com/xenafan/

This site is globally very fan-friendly, linking you up
to fan clubs all over the world. There's also a serviceable link to other *Xena* sites but the fan attitude is
this outlet's strong point.

The Bubba's Guide to Xena Warrior Princess
http://www.rampages.onramp.net/ccgddos/TXM/

This Texas-based Web site is totally gonzo. If you don't take *Xena* too seriously you'll laugh your chainmail bustier off at the wacked-out episode reviews and song parodies. Just plain fun.

The Ultimate Xena Episode Guide
http://www.members.aol.com/xenainfo/index.html

The title tells all. Concise story synopses of the first, second, and third seasons' episodes. A good way to catch up.

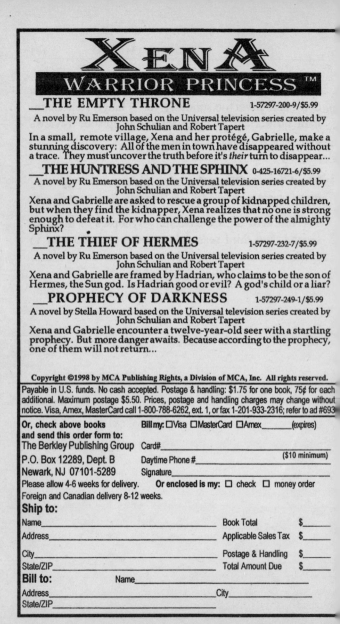

XENA
WARRIOR PRINCESS ™

___THE EMPTY THRONE   1-57297-200-9/$5.99

A novel by Ru Emerson based on the Universal television series created by
John Schulian and Robert Tapert

In a small, remote village, Xena and her protégé, Gabrielle, make a
stunning discovery: All of the men in town have disappeared without
a trace. They must uncover the truth before it's *their* turn to disappear...

___THE HUNTRESS AND THE SPHINX   0-425-16721-6/$5.99

A novel by Ru Emerson based on the Universal television series created by
John Schulian and Robert Tapert

Xena and Gabrielle are asked to rescue a group of kidnapped children,
but when they find the kidnapper, Xena realizes that no one is strong
enough to defeat it. For who can challenge the power of the almighty
Sphinx?

___THE THIEF OF HERMES   1-57297-232-7/$5.99

A novel by Ru Emerson based on the Universal television series created by
John Schulian and Robert Tapert

Xena and Gabrielle are framed by Hadrian, who claims to be the son of
Hermes, the Sun god. Is Hadrian good or evil? A god's child or a liar?

___PROPHECY OF DARKNESS   1-57297-249-1/$5.99

A novel by Stella Howard based on the Universal television series created by
John Schulian and Robert Tapert

Xena and Gabrielle encounter a twelve-year-old seer with a startling
prophecy. But more danger awaits. Because according to the prophecy,
one of them will not return...

Payable in U.S. funds. No cash accepted. Postage & handling: $1.75 for one book, 75¢ for each
additional. Maximum postage $5.50. Prices, postage and handling charges may change without
notice. Visa, Amex, MasterCard call 1-800-788-6262, ext. 1, or fax 1-201-933-2316; refer to ad #693

| Or, check above books
and send this order form to:
The Berkley Publishing Group

P.O. Box 12289, Dept. B
Newark, NJ 07101-5289 | Bill my: ☐Visa ☐MasterCard ☐Amex_____(expires)

Card#_____

Daytime Phone #_____ ($10 minimum)

Signature_____ |

Please allow 4-6 weeks for delivery.   **Or enclosed is my:** ☐ check ☐ money order
Foreign and Canadian delivery 8-12 weeks.

Ship to:

Name_____	Book Total	$_____
Address_____	Applicable Sales Tax	$_____
City_____	Postage & Handling	$_____
State/ZIP_____	Total Amount Due	$_____

Bill to: Name_____

Address_____City_____
State/ZIP_____